DOVER · THRIFT · EDITIONS

Short Stories

LOUISA MAY ALCOTT

DOVER PUBLICATIONS, INC.
New York

DOVER THRIFT EDITIONS

GENERAL EDITOR: STANLEY APPELBAUM
EDITOR OF THIS VOLUME: CANDACE WARD

Bibliographical Note

This Dover edition, first published in 1996, is a new collection of five stories by Louisa May Alcott. The texts are reprinted from the following sources: "Obtaining Supplies" and "A Night" (Chapters I and IV, respectively, of *Hospital Sketches*, Boston: James Redpath, 1863); "My Contraband" (*Hospital Sketches and Camp and Fireside Stories*, Boston: Roberts Bros., 1869); "Happy Women" (*The New York Ledger* 24, no. 7 [April 11, 1868]); "How I Went Out to Service" (*The Independent* 26, no. 1331 [June 4, 1874]). The introductory Note has been prepared specially for this edition.

Library of Congress Cataloging-in-Publication Data

Alcott, Louisa May, 1832–1888.
    Short stories / Louisa May Alcott.
        p.   cm. — (Dover thrift editions)
    Contents: From Hospital sketches: Obtaining supplies. A night — My contraband — Happy women — How I went out to service.
    ISBN 0-486-29063-8 (pbk.)
    1. United States—Social life and customs—19th century—Fiction. 2. United States—History—Civil War, 1861–1865—Women—Fiction. 3. Women—United States—Social life and customs—Fiction. 4. War stories, American. I. Title. II. Series.
PS1016   1996
813'.4—dc20   95-52418
                                                                                                          CIP

Manufactured in the United States of America
Dover Publications, Inc., 31 East 2nd Street, Mineola, N.Y. 11501

Note

LOUISA MAY ALCOTT (1832–1888) was born in Concord, Massachusetts, the daughter of Abigail May Alcott and Amos Bronson Alcott, the transcendental philosopher. Critics and biographers have pointed out Alcott's divided loyalties between her mother and father, and the tensions that arose from the latter's inability to provide for his family. Thoreau called Bronson Alcott a "great expecter," and another family friend observed that he "was a great feller for talkin' big . . . but his daughters is the gals though—always *doin'* somethin'" (Sam Staples, qtd. in Charles Ives, *Essays before a Sonata*). Louisa did more than "somethin'"—she became the family's financial mainstay with the money she earned writing fiction.

The success of *Little Women* (published in two volumes, 1868–69) and subsequent juvenile fiction, including *Little Men* (1871) and *Jo's Boys* (1886), ensured Alcott's reputation as a children's author. But Alcott's prose was not limited to what the composer Charles Ives referred to as the "wholesome thoughts" and "wholesome emotions" contained in her children's books. Over the past fifty years scholars have discovered a number of Alcott's sensational, sometimes lurid, melo-dramas published anonymously in journals such as *Frank Leslie's Illustrated Newspaper* and *Frank Leslie's Lady's Magazine*. These stories, with titles such as "Doctor Dorn's Revenge" and "My Mysterious Mademoiselle," were written during a period of intense literary activity. As Madeleine B. Stern notes, during the decade of the 1860s Alcott produced other thrillers for *Frank Leslie's Chimney Corner,* stories for the *Flag of Our Union, Putnam's Magazine* and the children's magazine *Merry's Museum* (which she edited from 1866 to 1870), as well as *Little Women.*

Four of the five stories reprinted here were written during this period. "Obtaining Supplies" and "A Night" are based on Alcott's experiences as a volunteer nurse during the Civil War. Like her narrator Tribulation Periwinkle, Alcott traveled from New England to Washington to serve in a Georgetown military hospital. Alcott's nursing career lasted six weeks, until she contracted typhoid fever and had to return to Concord. These autobiographical sketches were originally published in a Boston abolitionist paper, and in 1863 they were collected in *Hospital Sketches.* "My Contraband" was first published in an 1863 issue of the *Atlantic Monthly.* It, too, is set in a military hospital, though in this tale Alcott's heroine is called on to nurse a Confederate prisoner. The dramatic tension between the Rebel officer, his ex-slave (and half-brother) and Nurse Dane is similar to the exaggerated tensions in Alcott's anonymous thrillers, but the drama of "My Contraband" is balanced by the realism that characterizes all of Alcott's autobiographical fiction.

"Happy Women" and "How I Went Out to Service" explore issues that Alcott faced in her private life. The former, written in 1868 when Alcott was 36 years old, is a short sketch warning young women against rushing into matrimony: "the loss of liberty, happiness, and self-respect is poorly repaid by the barren honor of being called 'Mrs.' instead of 'Miss.'" Alcott's ambivalence about matrimony is partly attributable to the inequities she perceived in her parents' marriage and her own experiences living as a single woman at a time when women were expected to marry. The women Alcott describes provide a counterpoint to conventional representations of nineteenth-century women; "L.," "M.," "S." and "A." are made happy by their work and the satisfaction they derive from it. The question of women and work was a major concern for Alcott, and she presents a humorous account of her early bid for independence as a household servant in "How I Went Out to Service." The humor, however, does not diminish Alcott's criticism of her society's limited employment opportunities for women.

Contents

From *Hospital Sketches*

I. Obtaining Supplies

"I WANT SOMETHING to do."

This remark being addressed to the world in general, no one in particular felt it their duty to reply; so I repeated it to the smaller world about me, received the following suggestions, and settled the matter by answering my own inquiry, as people are apt to do when very much in earnest.

"Write a book," quoth the author of my being.

"Don't know enough, sir. First live, then write."

"Try teaching again," suggested mother.

"No thank you, ma'am, ten years of that is enough."

"Take a husband like my Darby, and fulfill your mission," said sister Joan, home on a visit.

"Can't afford expensive luxuries, Mrs. Coobiddy."

"Turn actress, and immortalize your name," said sister Vashti, striking an attitude.

"I won't."

"Go nurse the soldiers," said my young brother, Tom, panting for "the tented field."

"I will!"

So far, very good. Here was the will—now for the way. At first sight not a foot of it appeared, but that didn't matter, for the Periwinkles are a hopeful race; their crest is an anchor, with three cock-a-doodles crowing atop. They all wear rose-colored spectacles, and are lineal descendants of the inventor of aerial architecture. An hour's conversation on the subject set the whole family in a blaze of enthusiasm. A model hospital was erected, and each member had accepted an honorable post therein. The paternal P. was chaplain, the maternal P. was matron, and all the youthful P.s filled the pod of futurity with achievements whose brilliancy eclipsed the glories of the present and the past. Arriving at this satisfactory conclusion, the meeting adjourned, and the fact that Miss Tribulation was available as army nurse went abroad on the wings of the wind.

1

In a few days a townswoman heard of my desire, approved of it, and brought about an interview with one of the sisterhood which I wished to join, who was at home on a furlough, and able and willing to satisfy all inquiries. A morning chat with Miss General S.—we hear no end of Mrs. Generals, why not a Miss?—produced three results: I felt that I could do the work, was offered a place, and accepted it, promising not to desert, but stand ready to march on Washington at an hour's notice.

A few days were necessary for the letter containing my request and recommendation to reach headquarters, and another, containing my commission, to return; therefore no time was to be lost; and heartily thanking my pair of friends, I tore home through the December slush as if the rebels were after me, and like many another recruit, burst in upon my family with the announcement—

"I've enlisted!"

An impressive silence followed. Tom, the irrepressible, broke it with a slap on the shoulder and the graceful compliment—

"Old Trib, you're a trump!"

"Thank you; then I'll *take* something:" which I did, in the shape of dinner, reeling off my news at the rate of three dozen words to a mouthful; and as everyone else talked equally fast, and all together, the scene was most inspiring.

As boys going to sea immediately become nautical in speech, walk as if they already had their "sea legs" on, and shiver their timbers on all possible occasions, so I turned military at once, called my dinner my rations, saluted all new comers, and ordered a dress parade that very afternoon. Having reviewed every rag I possessed, I detailed some for picket duty while airing over the fence; some to the sanitary influences of the wash-tub; others to mount guard in the trunk; while the weak and wounded went to the Work-basket Hospital, to be made ready for active service again. To this squad I devoted myself for a week; but all was done, and I had time to get powerfully impatient before the letter came. It did arrive however, and brought a disappointment along with its good will and friendliness, for it told me that the place in the Armory Hospital that I supposed I was to take, was already filled, and a much less desirable one at Hurly-burly House was offered instead.

"That's just your luck, Trib. I'll tote your trunk up garret for you again; for of course you won't go," Tom remarked, with the disdainful pity which small boys affect when they get into their teens. I was wavering in my secret soul, but that settled the matter, and I crushed him on the spot with martial brevity—

"It is now one; I shall march at six."

I have a confused recollection of spending the afternoon in pervading the house like an executive whirlwind, with my family swarming after me, all working, talking, prophesying and lamenting, while I packed my "go-abroady" possessions, tumbled the rest into two big boxes, danced on the lids till they shut, and gave them in charge, with the direction,—

"If I never come back, make a bonfire of them."

Then I choked down a cup of tea, generously salted instead of sugared, by some agitated relative, shouldered my knapsack—it was only a traveling bag, but do let me preserve the unities—hugged my family three times all round without a vestige of unmanly emotion, till a certain dear old lady broke down upon my neck, with a despairing sort of wail—

"Oh, my dear, my dear, how can I let you go?"

"I'll stay if you say so, mother."

"But I don't; go, and the Lord will take care of you."

Much of the Roman matron's courage had gone into the Yankee matron's composition, and, in spite of her tears, she would have sent ten sons to the war, had she possessed them, as freely as she sent one daughter, smiling and flapping on the door-step till I vanished, though the eyes that followed me were very dim, and the handkerchief she waved was very wet.

My transit from The Gables to the village depot was a funny mixture of good wishes and good byes, mud-puddles and shopping. A December twilight is not the most cheering time to enter upon a somewhat perilous enterprise, and, but for the presence of Vashti and neighbor Thorn, I fear that I might have added a drop of the briny to the native moisture of—

"The town I left behind me;"

though I'd no thought of giving out: oh, bless you, no! When the engine screeched "Here we are," I clutched my escort in a fervent embrace, and skipped into the car with as blithe a farewell as if going on a bridal tour—though I believe brides don't usually wear cavernous black bonnets and fuzzy brown coats, with a hair-brush, a pair of rubbers, two books, and a bag of ginger-bread distorting the pockets of the same. If I thought that any one would believe it, I'd boldly state that I slept from C. to B., which would simplify matters immensely; but as I know they wouldn't, I'll confess that the head under the funereal coal-hod fermented with all manner of high thoughts and heroic purposes "to do or die,"—perhaps both; and the heart under the fuzzy brown coat felt very tender with the memory of the dear old lady, probably sobbing over her army socks and the loss of her topsy-turvy Trib. At this juncture I took the veil, and what I did behind it is nobody's business; but I maintain that the soldier who cries when his mother says "Good bye," is the boy to fight best, and die bravest, when the time comes, or go back to her better than he went.

Till nine o'clock I trotted about the city streets, doing those last errands which no woman would even go to heaven without attempting, if she could. Then I went to my usual refuge, and, fully intending to keep awake, as a sort of vigil appropriate to the occasion, fell fast asleep and dreamed propitious dreams till my rosy-faced cousin waked me with a kiss.

A bright day smiled upon my enterprise, and at ten I reported myself to my General, received last instructions and no end of the sympathetic encouragement which women give, in look, touch, and tone more effectually than in words. The next step was to get a free pass to Washington, for I'd no desire to waste my substance on railroad companies when "the boys" needed even a spinster's mite. A friend of mine had procured such a pass, and I was bent on doing likewise, though I had to face the president of the railroad to accomplish it. I'm a bashful individual, though I can't get any one to believe it; so it cost me a great effort to poke about the Worcester depot till the right door appeared, then walk into a room containing several gentlemen, and blunder out my request in a high state of stammer and blush. Nothing could have been more courteous than this dreaded President, but it was evident that I had made as absurd a demand as-if I had asked for the nose off his respectable face. He referred me to the Governor at the State House, and I backed out, leaving him no doubt to regret that such mild maniacs were left at large. Here was a Scylla and Charybdis business: as if a President wasn't trying enough, without the Governor of Massachusetts and the hub of the hub piled on top of that. "I never can do it," thought I. "Tom will hoot at you if you don't," whispered the inconvenient little voice that is always goading people to the performance of disagreeable duties, and always appeals to the most effective agent to produce the proper result. The idea of allowing any boy that ever wore a felt basin and a shoddy jacket with a microscopic tail, to crow over me, was preposterous, so giving myself a mental slap for such faint-heartedness, I streamed away across the Common, wondering if I ought to say "your Honor," or simply "Sir," and decided upon the latter, fortifying myself with recollections of an evening in a charming green library, where I beheld the Governor placidly consuming oysters, and laughing as if Massachusetts was a myth, and he had no heavier burden on his shoulders than his host's handsome hands.

Like an energetic fly in a very large cobweb, I struggled through the State House, getting into all the wrong rooms and none of the right, till I turned desperate, and went into one, resolving not to come out till I'd made somebody hear and answer me. I suspect that of all the wrong places I had blundered into, this was the most so. But I didn't care; and, though the apartment was full of soldiers, surgeons, starers, and spittoons, I cornered a perfectly incapable person, and proceeded to pump for information with the following result:

"Was the Governor anywhere about?"

No, he wasn't.

"Could he tell me where to look?"

No, he couldn't.

"Did he know anything about free passes?"

No, he didn't.

"Was there any one there of whom I could inquire?"

Not a person.

"Did he know of any place where information could be obtained?"

Not a place.

"Could he throw the smallest gleam of light upon the matter, in any way?"

Not a ray.

I am naturally irascible, and if I could have shaken this negative gentleman vigorously, the relief would have been immense. The prejudices of society forbidding this mode of redress, I merely glowered at him; and, before my wrath found vent in words, my General appeared, having seen me from an opposite window, and come to know what I was about. At her command the languid gentleman woke up, and troubled himself to remember that Major or Sergeant or something Mc K. knew all about the tickets, and his office was in Milk Street. I perked up instanter, and then, as if the exertion was too much for him, what did this animated wet blanket do but add—

"I think Mc K. may have left Milk Street, now, and I don't know where he has gone."

"Never mind; the new comers will know where he has moved to, my dear, so don't be discouraged; and if you don't succeed, come to me, and we will see what to do next," said my General.

I blessed her in a fervent manner and a cool hall, fluttered round the corner, and bore down Milk Street, bent on discovering Mc K. if such a being was to be found. He wasn't, and the ignorance of the neighborhood was really pitiable. Nobody knew anything, and after tumbling over bundles of leather, bumping against big boxes, being nearly annihilated by descending bales, and sworn at by aggravated truckmen,

I finally elicited the advice to look for Mc K. in Haymarket Square. Who my informant was I've really forgotten; for, having hailed several busy gentlemen, some one of them fabricated this delusive quietus for the perturbed spirit, who instantly departed to the sequestered locality he named. If I had been in search of the Koh-i-noor diamond I should have been as likely to find it there as any vestige of Mc K. I stared at signs, inquired in shops, invaded an eating house, visited the recruiting tent in the middle of the Square, made myself a nuisance generally, and accumulated mud enough to retard another Nile. All in vain: and I mournfully turned my face toward the General's, feeling that I should be forced to enrich the railroad company after all; when, suddenly, I beheld that admirable young man, brother-in-law Darby Coobiddy, Esq. I arrested him with a burst of news, and wants, and woes, which caused his manly countenance to lose its usual repose.

"Oh, my dear boy, I'm going to Washington at five, and I can't find the free ticket man, and there won't be time to see Joan, and I'm so tired and cross I don't know what to do; and will you help me, like a cherub as you are?"

"Oh, yes, of course. I know a fellow who will set us right," responded Darby, mildly excited, and darting into some kind of an office, held counsel with an invisible angel, who sent him out radiant. "All serene. I've got him. I'll see you through the business, and then get Joan from the Dove Cote in time to see you off."

I'm a woman's rights woman, and if any man had offered help in the morning, I should have condescendingly refused it, sure that I could do everything as well, if not better, myself. My strong-mindedness had rather abated since then, and I was now quite ready to be a "timid trembler," if necessary. Dear me! how easily Darby did it all: he just asked one question, received an answer, tucked me under his arm, and in ten minutes I stood in the presence of Mc K., the Desired.

"Now my troubles are over," thought I, and as usual was direfully mistaken.

"You will have to get a pass from Dr. H., in Temple Place, before I can give you a pass, madam," answered Mc K., as blandly as if he wasn't carrying desolation to my soul. Oh, indeed! why didn't he send me to Dorchester Heights, India Wharf, or Bunker Hill Monument, and done with it? Here I was, after a morning's tramp, down in some place about Dock Square, and was told to step to Temple Place. Nor was that all; he might as well have asked me to catch a humming-bird, toast a salamander, or call on the man in the moon, as find a Doctor at home at the busiest hour of the day. It was a blow; but weariness had extinguished enthusiasm, and resignation clothed me as a garment. I sent Darby for Joan, and doggedly paddled off, feeling that mud was my native element, and quite sure that the evening papers would announce the appearance of the Wandering Jew, in feminine habiliments.

"Is Dr. H. in?"

"No, mum, he aint."

Of course he wasn't; I knew that before I asked: and, considering it all in the light of a hollow mockery, added:

"When will he probably return?"

If the damsel had said, "ten to-night," I should have felt a grim satisfaction, in the fulfillment of my own dark prophecy; but she said, "At two, mum;" and I felt it a personal insult.

"I'll call, then. Tell him my business is important:" with which mysteriously delivered message I departed, hoping that I left her consumed with curiosity; for mud rendered me an object of interest.

By way of resting myself, I crossed the Common, for the third time, bespoke the carriage, got some lunch, packed my purchases, smoothed my plumage, and was back again, as the clock struck two. The Doctor hadn't come yet; and I was morally certain that he would not, till, having waited till the last minute, I was driven to buy a ticket, and, five minutes after the irrevocable deed was done, he would be at my service, with all manner of helpful documents and directions. Everything goes by contraries with me; so, having made up my mind to be disappointed, of course I wasn't; for, presently, in walked Dr. H., and no sooner had he heard my errand, and glanced at my credentials, than he said, with the most engaging readiness:

"I will give you the order, with pleasure, madam."

Words cannot express how soothing and delightful it was to find, at last, somebody who could do what I wanted, without sending me from Dan to Beersheba, for a dozen other bodies to do something else first. Peace descended, like oil, upon the ruffled waters of my being, as I sat listening to the busy scratch of his pen; and, when he turned about, giving me not only the order, but a paper of directions wherewith to smooth away all difficulties between Boston and Washington, I felt as did poor Christian when the Evangelist gave him the scroll, on the safe side of the Slough of Despond. I've no doubt many dismal nurses have inflicted themselves upon the worthy gentleman since then; but I am sure none have been more kindly helped, or are more grateful, than T. P.; for that short interview added another to the many pleasant associations that already surround his name.

Feeling myself no longer a "Martha Struggles," but a comfortable young woman, with plain sailing before her, and the worst of the voyage well over, I once more presented myself to the valuable Mc K. The order was read, and certain printed papers, necessary to be filled out, were given a young gentleman—no, I prefer to say Boy, with a scornful emphasis upon the word, as the only means of revenge now left me. This Boy, instead of doing his duty with the diligence so charming in the young, loitered and lounged, in a manner which proved his education to have been sadly neglected in the—

> "How doth the little busy bee,"

direction. He stared at me, gaped out of the window, ate peanuts, and gossiped with his neighbors—Boys, like himself, and all penned in a row, like colts at a Cattle Show. I don't imagine he knew the anguish he was inflicting; for it was nearly three, the train left at five, and I had my ticket to get, my dinner to eat, my blessed sister to see, and the depot to reach, if I didn't die of apoplexy. Meanwhile, Patience certainly had her perfect work that day, and I hope she enjoyed the job more than I did. Having waited some twenty minutes, it pleased this reprehensible Boy to make varous marks and blots on my documents, toss them to a venerable creature of sixteen, who delivered them to me with such paternal directions, that it only needed a pat on the head and an encouraging—"Now run home to your Ma, little girl, and mind the crossings, my dear," to make the illusion quite perfect.

Why I was sent to a steamboat office for car tickets, is not for me to say, though I went as meekly as I should have gone to the Probate Court, if sent. A fat, easy gentleman gave me several bits of paper, with coupons attached, with a warning not to separate them, which instantly inspired me with a yearning to pluck them apart, and see what came of it. But, remembering through what fear and tribulation I had obtained them, I curbed Satan's promptings, and, clutching my prize, as if it were my pass to the Elysian Fields, I hurried home. Dinner was rapidly consumed; Joan enlightened, comforted, and kissed; the dearest of apple-faced cousins hugged; the kindest of apple-faced cousins' fathers subjected to the same process; and I mounted the ambulance, baggage-wagon, or anything you please but hack, and drove away, too tired to feel excited, sorry, or glad.

From *Hospital Sketches*

IV. A Night

BEING FOND OF the night side of nature, I was soon promoted to the post of night nurse, with every facility for indulging in my favorite pastime of "owling." My colleague, a black-eyed widow, relieved me at dawn, we two taking care of the ward between us, like regular nurses, turn and turn about. I usually found my boys in the jolliest state of mind their condition allowed; for it was a known fact that Nurse Periwinkle objected to blue devils, and entertained a belief that he who laughed most was surest of recovery. At the beginning of my reign, dumps and dismals prevailed; the nurses looked anxious and tired, the men gloomy or sad; and a general "Hark! from-the-tombs-a-doleful-sound" style of conversation seemed to be the fashion: a state of things which caused one coming from a merry, social New England town, to feel as if she had got into an exhausted receiver; and the instinct of self-preservation, to say nothing of a philanthropic desire to serve the race, caused a speedy change in Ward No. 1.

More flattering than the most gracefully turned compliment, more grateful than the most admiring glance, was the sight of those rows of faces, all strange to me a little while ago, now lighting up, with smiles of welcome, as I came among them, enjoying that moment heartily, with a womanly pride in their regard, a motherly affection for them all. The evenings were spent in reading aloud, writing letters, waiting on and amusing the men, going the rounds with Dr. P., as he made his second daily survey, dressing my dozen wounds afresh, giving last doses, and making them cozy for the long hours to come, till the nine o'clock bell rang, the gas was turned down, the day nurses went off duty, the night watch came on, and my nocturnal adventures began.

My ward was now divided into three rooms; and, under favor of the matron, I had managed to sort out the patients in such a way that I had what I called, "my duty room," my "pleasure room," and my "pathetic room," and worked for each in a different way. One, I visited, armed with a dressing tray, full of rollers, plasters, and pins; another, with books, flowers, games, and gossip; a third, with teapots, lullabies, consolation, and, sometimes, a shroud.

Wherever the sickest or most helpless man chanced to be, there I held my watch, often visiting the other rooms, to see that the general watchman of the ward did his duty by the fires and the wounds, the latter needing constant wetting. Not only on this account did I meander, but also to get fresher air than the close rooms afforded; for, owing to the stupidity of that mysterious "somebody" who does all the damage in the world, the windows had been carefully nailed down above, and the lower sashes could only be raised in the mildest weather, for the men lay just below. I had suggested a summary smashing of a few panes here and there, when frequent appeals to headquarters had proved unavailing, and daily orders to lazy attendants had come to nothing. No one seconded the motion, however, and the nails were far beyond my reach; for, though belonging to the sisterhood of "ministering angels," I had no wings, and might as well have asked for a suspension bridge, as a pair of steps, in that charitable chaos.

One of the harmless ghosts who bore me company during the haunted hours, was Dan, the watchman, whom I regarded with a certain awe; for, though so much together, I never fairly saw his face, and, but for his legs, should never have recognized him, as we seldom met by day. These legs were remarkable, as was his whole figure, for his body was short, rotund, and done up in a big jacket, and muffler; his beard hid the lower part of his face, his hat-brim the upper; and all I ever discovered was a pair of sleepy eyes, and a very mild voice. But the legs!—very long, very thin, very crooked and feeble, looking like gray sausages in their tight coverings, and finished off with a pair of expansive, green cloth shoes, very like Chinese junks with the sails down. This figure, gliding noiselessly about the dimly-lighted rooms, was strongly suggestive of the spirit of a beer-barrel mounted on cork-screws, haunting the old hotel in search of its lost mates, emptied and staved in long ago.

Another goblin who frequently appeared to me, was the attendant of "the pathetic room," who, being a faithful soul, was often up to tend two or three men, weak and wandering as babies, after the fever had gone. The amiable creature beguiled the watches of the night by brewing jorums of a fearful beverage, which he called coffee, and insisted on sharing with me; coming in with a great bowl of something like mud soup, scalding hot, guiltless of cream, rich in an all-pervading flavor of molasses, scorch and tin pot. Such an amount of good will and neighborly kindness also went into the mess, that I never could find the heart to refuse, but always received it with thanks, sipped it with hypocritical relish while he remained, and whipped it into the slop-jar the instant he departed, thereby gratifying him, securing one rousing laugh in the doziest hour of the night, and no one was the worse for the transaction but the pigs. Whether they were "cut off untimely in their sins," or not, I carefully abstained from inquiring.

It was a strange life—asleep half the day, exploring Washington the other half, and all night hovering, like a massive cherubim, in a red rigolette, over the slumbering sons of man. I liked it, and found many things to amuse, instruct, and interest me. The snores alone were quite a study, varying from the mild sniff to the stentorian snort, which startled the echoes and hoisted the performer erect to accuse his neighbor of the deed, magnanimously forgive him, and, wrapping the drapery of his couch about him, lie down to vocal slumber. After listening for a week to this band of wind instruments, I indulged in the belief that I could recognize each by the snore alone, and was tempted to join the chorus by breaking out with John Brown's favorite hymn:

"Blow ye the trumpet, blow!"

I would have given much to have possessed the art of sketching, for many of the faces became wonderfully interesting when unconscious. Some grew stern and grim, the men evidently dreaming of war, as they gave orders, groaned over their wounds, or damned the rebels vigorously; some grew sad and infinitely pathetic, as if the pain borne silently all day, revenged itself by now betraying what the man's pride had concealed so well. Often the roughest grew young and pleasant when sleep smoothed the hard lines away, letting the real nature assert itself; many almost seemed to speak, and I learned to know these men better by night than through any intercourse by day. Sometimes they disappointed me, for faces that looked merry and good in the light, grew bad and sly when the shadows came; and though they made no confidences in words, I read their lives, leaving them to wonder at the change of manner this midnight magic wrought in their nurse. A few talked busily; one drummer boy sang sweetly, though no persuasions could win a note from him by day; and several depended on being told what they had talked of in the morning. Even my constitutionals in the chilly halls, possessed a certain charm, for the house was never still. Sentinels tramped round it all night long, their muskets glittering in the wintry moonlight as they walked, or stood before the doors, straight and silent, as figures of stone, causing one to conjure up romantic visions of guarded forts, sudden surprises, and daring deeds; for in these war times

the hum drum life of Yankeedom has vanished, and the most prosaic
feel some thrill of that excitement which stirs the nation's heart, and
makes its capital a camp of hospitals. Wandering up and down these
lower halls, I often heard cries from above, steps hurrying to and fro, saw
surgeons passing up, or men coming down carrying a stretcher, where
lay a long white figure, whose face was shrouded and whose fight was
done. Sometimes I stopped to watch the passers in the street, the
moonlight shining on the spire opposite, or the gleam of some vessel
floating, like a white-winged sea-gull, down the broad Potomac, whose
fullest flow can never wash away the red stain of the land.

The night whose events I have a fancy to record, opened with a little
comedy, and closed with a great tragedy; for a virtuous and useful life
untimely ended is always tragical to those who see not as God sees. My
headquarters were beside the bed of a New Jersey boy, crazed by the
horrors of that dreadful Saturday. A slight wound in the knee brought
him there; but his mind had suffered more than his body; some string of
that delicate machine was over strained, and, for days, he had been
re-living in imagination, the scenes he could not forget, till his distress
broke out in incoherent ravings, pitiful to hear. As I sat by him,
endeavoring to soothe his poor distracted brain by the constant touch of
wet hands over his hot forehead, he lay cheering his comrades on,
hurrying them back, then counting them as they fell around him, often
clutching my arm, to drag me from the vicinity of a bursting shell, or
covering up his head to screen himself from a shower of shot; his face
brilliant with fever; his eyes restless; his head never still; every muscle
strained and rigid; while an incessant stream of defiant shouts,
whispered warnings, and broken laments, poured from his lips with that
forceful bewilderment which makes such wanderings so hard to
overhear.

It was past eleven, and my patient was slowly wearying himself into
fitful intervals of quietude, when, in one of these pauses, a curious
sound arrested my attention. Looking over my shoulder, I saw a one-
legged phantom hopping nimbly down the room; and, going to meet it,
recognized a certain Pennsylvania gentleman, whose wound-fever had
taken a turn for the worse, and, depriving him of the few wits a drunken
campaign had left him, set him literally tripping on the light, fantastic
toe "toward home," as he blandly informed me, touching the military
cap which formed a striking contrast to the severe simplicity of the rest
of his *undress* uniform. When sane, the least movement produced a roar
of pain or a volley of oaths; but the departure of reason seemed to have

wrought an agreeable change, both in the man and his manners; for, balancing himself on one leg, like a meditative stork, he plunged into an animated discussion of the war, the President, lager beer, and Enfield rifles, regardless of any suggestions of mine as to the propriety of returning to bed, lest he be court-martialed for desertion.

Any thing more supremely ridiculous can hardly be imagined than this figure, all draped in white, its one foot covered with a big blue sock, a dingy cap set rakingly askew on its shaven head, and placid satisfaction beaming in its broad red face, as it flourished a mug in one hand, an old boot in the other, calling them canteen and knapsack, while it skipped and fluttered in the most unearthly fashion. What to do with the creature I didn't know; Dan was absent, and if I went to find him, the perambulator might festoon himself out of the window, set his toga on fire, or do some of his neighbors a mischief. The attendant of the room was sleeping like a near relative of the celebrated Seven, and nothing short of pins would rouse him; for he had been out that day, and whiskey asserted its supremacy in balmy whiffs. Still declaiming, in a fine flow of eloquence, the demented gentleman hopped on, blind and deaf to my graspings and entreaties; and I was about to slam the door in his face, and run for help, when a second and saner phantom came to the rescue, in the likeness of a big Prussian, who spoke no English, but divined the crisis, and put an end to it, by bundling the lively monoped into his bed, like a baby, with an authoritative command to "stay put," which received added weight from being delivered in an odd con-glomeration of French and German, accompanied by warning wags of a head decorated with a yellow cotton night cap, rendered most imposing by a tassel like a bell-pull. Rather exhausted by his excursion, the member from Pennsylvania subsided; and, after an irrepressible laugh together, my Prussian ally and myself were returning to our places, when the echo of a sob caused us to glance along the beds. It came from one in the corner—such a little bed!—and such a tearful little face looked up at us, as we stopped beside it! The twelve years old drummer boy was not singing now, but sobbing, with a manly effort all the while to stifle the distressful sounds that would break out.

"What is it, Billy?" I asked, as he rubbed the tears away, and checked himself in the middle of a great sob to answer plaintively:

"I've got a chill, ma'am, but I aint cryin' for that, 'cause I'm used to it. I dreamed Kit was here, and when I waked up he wasn't, and I couldn't help it, then."

The boy came in with the rest, and the man who was taken dead from the ambulance was the Kit he mourned. Well he might; for, when the wounded were brought from Fredericksburg, the child lay in one of the camps thereabout, and this good friend, though sorely hurt himself, would not leave him to the exposure and neglect of such a time and place; but, wrapping him in his own blanket, carried him in his arms to the transport, tended him during the passage, and only yielded up his charge when Death met him at the door of the hospital which promised care and comfort for the boy. For ten days, Billy had burned or shivered with fever and ague, pining the while for Kit, and refusing to be comforted, because he had not been able to thank him for the generous protection, which, perhaps, had cost the giver's life. The vivid dream had wrung the childish heart with a fresh pang, and when I tried the solace fitted for his years, the remorseful fear that haunted him found vent in a fresh burst of tears, as he looked at the wasted hands I was endeavoring to warm:

"Oh! if I'd only been as thin when Kit carried me as I am now, maybe he wouldn't have died; but I was heavy, he was hurt worser than we knew, and so it killed him; and I didn't see him, to say good bye."

This thought had troubled him in secret; and my assurances that his friend would probably have died at all events, hardly assuaged the bitterness of his regretful grief.

At this juncture, the delirious man began to shout; the one-legged rose up in his bed, as if preparing for another dart, Billy bewailed himself more piteously than before: and if ever a woman was at her wit's end, that distracted female was Nurse Periwinkle, during the space of two or three minutes, as she vibrated between the three beds, like an agitated pendulum. Like a most opportune reinforcement, Dan, the bandy, appeared, and devoted himself to the lively party, leaving me free to return to my post; for the Prussian, with a nod and a smile, took the lad away to his own bed, and lulled him to sleep with a soothing murmur, like a mammoth humble bee. I liked that in Fritz, and if he ever wondered afterward at the dainties which sometimes found their way into his rations, or the extra comforts of his bed, he might have found a solution of the mystery in sundry persons' knowledge of the fatherly action of that night.

Hardly was I settled again, when the inevitable bowl appeared, and its bearer delivered a message I had expected, yet dreaded to receive:

"John is going, ma'am, and wants to see you, if you can come."

"The moment this boy is asleep; tell him so, and let me know if I am in danger of being too late."

My Ganymede departed, and while I quieted poor Shaw, I thought of John. He came in a day or two after the others; and, one evening, when I entered my "pathetic room," I found a lately emptied bed occupied by a large, fair man, with a fine face, and the serenest eyes I ever met. One of the earlier comers had often spoken of a friend, who had remained behind, that those apparently worse wounded than himself might reach a shelter first. It seemed a David and Jonathan sort of friendship. The man fretted for his mate, and was never tired of praising John—his courage, sobriety, self-denial, and unfailing kindliness of heart; always winding up with: "He's an out an' out fine feller, ma'am; you see if he aint."

I had some curiosity to behold this piece of excellence, and when he came, watched him for a night or two, before I made friends with him; for, to tell the truth, I was a little afraid of the stately looking man, whose bed had to be lengthened to accommodate his commanding stature; who seldom spoke, uttered no complaint, asked no sympathy, but tranquilly observed what went on about him; and, as he lay high upon his pillows, no picture of dying statesman or warrior was ever fuller of real dignity than this Virginia blacksmith. A most attractive face he had, framed in brown hair and beard, comely featured and full of vigor, as yet unsubdued by pain; thoughtful and often beautifully mild while watching the afflictions of others, as if entirely forgetful of his own. His mouth was grave and firm, with plenty of will and courage in its lines, but a smile could make it as sweet as any woman's; and his eyes were child's eyes, looking one fairly in the face, with a clear, straightforward glance, which promised well for such as placed their faith in him. He seemed to cling to life, as if it were rich in duties and delights, and he had learned the secret of content. The only time I saw his composure disturbed, was when my surgeon brought another to examine John, who scrutinized their faces with an anxious look, asking of the elder: "Do you think I shall pull through, sir?" "I hope so, my man." And, as the two passed on, John's eye still followed them, with an intentness which would have won a truer answer from them, had they seen it. A momentary shadow flitted over his face; then came the usual serenity, as if, in that brief eclipse, he had acknowledged the existence of some hard possibility, and, asking nothing yet hoping all things, left the issue in God's hands, with that submission which is true piety.

The next night, as I went by rounds with Dr. P., I happened to ask which man in the room probably suffered most; and, to my great surprise, he glanced at John:

"Every breath he draws is like a stab; for the ball pierced the left lung, broke a rib, and did no end of damage here and there; so the poor lad can find neither forgetfulness nor ease, because he must lie on his wounded back or suffocate. It will be a hard struggle, and a long one, for he posseses great vitality; but even his temperate life can't save him; I wish it could."

"You don't mean he must die, Doctor?"

"Bless you, there's not the slightest hope for him; and you'd better tell him so before long; women have a way of doing such things comfortably, so I leave it to you. He won't last more than a day or two, at furthest."

I could have sat down on the spot and cried heartily, if I had not learned the wisdom of bottling up one's tears for leisure moments. Such an end seemed very hard for such a man, when half a dozen worn out, worthless bodies round him, were gathering up the remnants of wasted lives, to linger on for years perhaps, burdens to others, daily reproaches to themselves. The army needed men like John, earnest, brave, and faithful; fighting for liberty and justice with both heart and hand, true soldiers of the Lord. I could not give him up so soon, or think with any patience of so excellent a nature robbed of its fulfillment, and blundered into eternity by the rashness or stupidity of those at whose hands so many lives may be required. It was an easy thing for Dr. P. to say: "Tell him he must die," but a cruelly hard thing to do, and by no means as "comfortable" as he politely suggested. I had not the heart to do it then, and privately indulged the hope that some change for the better might take place, in spite of gloomy prophesies; so, rendering my task unnecessary.

A few minutes later, as I came in again, with fresh rollers, I saw John sitting erect, with no one to support him, while the surgeon dressed his back. I had never hitherto seen it done; for, having simpler wounds to attend to, and knowing the fidelity of the attendant, I had left John to him, thinking it might be more agreeable and safe; for both strength and experience were needed in his case. I had forgotten that the strong man might long for the gentle tendance of a woman's hands, the sympathetic magnetism of a woman's presence, as well as the feebler souls about him. The Doctor's words caused me to reproach myself with neglect, not of any real duty perhaps, but of those little cares and kindnesses that solace homesick spirits, and make the heavy hours pass easier. John looked lonely and forsaken just then, as he sat with bent head, hands folded on his knee, and no outward sign of suffering, till, looking nearer,

I saw great tears roll down and drop upon the floor. It was a new sight there; for, though I had seen many suffer, some swore, some groaned, most endured silently, but none wept. Yet it did not seem weak, only very touching, and straightway my fear vanished, my heart opened wide and took him in, as, gathering the bent head in my arms, as freely as if he had been a little child, I said, "Let me help you bear it, John."

Never, on any human countenance, have I seen so swift and beautiful a look of gratitude, surprise and comfort, as that which answered me more eloquently than the whispered—

"Thank you, ma'am, this is right good! this is what I wanted!"

"Then why not ask for it before?"

"I didn't like to be a trouble; you seemed so busy, and I could manage to get on alone."

"You shall not want it any more, John."

Nor did he; for now I understood the wistful look that sometimes followed me, as I went out, after a brief pause beside his bed, or merely a passing nod, while busied with those who seemed to need me more than he, because more urgent in their demands. Now I knew that to him, as to so many, I was the poor substitute for mother, wife, or sister, and in his eyes no stranger, but a friend who hitherto had seemed neglectful; for, in his modesty, he had never guessed the truth. This was changed now; and, through the tedious operation of probing, bathing, and dressing his wounds, he leaned against me, holding my hand fast, and, if pain wrung further tears from him, no one saw them fall but me. When he was laid down again, I hovered about him, in a remorseful state of mind that would not let me rest, till I had bathed his face, brushed his bonny brown hair, set all things smooth about him, and laid a knot of heath and heliotrope on his clean pillow. While doing this, he watched me with the satisfied expression I so liked to see; and when I offered the little nosegay, held it carefully in his great hand, smoothed a ruffled leaf or two, surveyed and smelt it with an air of genuine delight, and lay contentedly regarding the glimmer of the sunshine on the green. Although the manliest man among my forty, he said, "Yes, ma'am," like a little boy; received suggestions for his comfort with the quick smile that brightened his whole face; and now and then, as I stood tidying the table by his bed, I felt him softly touch my gown, as if to assure himself that I was there. Anything more natural and frank I never saw, and found this brave John as bashful as brave, yet full of excellencies and fine aspirations, which, having no power to express themselves in words, seemed to have bloomed into his character and made him what he was.

After that night, an hour of each evening that remained to him was devoted to his ease or pleasure. He could not talk much, for breath was precious, and he spoke in whispers; but from occasional conversations, I gleaned scraps of private history which only added to the affection and respect I felt for him. Once he asked me to write a letter, and as I settled pen and paper, I said, with an irrepressible glimmer of feminine curiosity, "Shall it be addressed to wife, or mother, John?"

"Neither, ma'am; I've got no wife, and will write to mother myself when I get better. Did you think I was married because of this?" he asked, touching a plain ring he wore, and often turned thoughtfully on his finger when he lay alone.

"Partly that, but more from a settled sort of look you have; a look which young men seldom get until they marry."

"I didn't know that; but I'm not so very young, ma'am, thirty in May, and have been what you might call settled this ten years. Mother's a widow, I'm the oldest child she has, and it wouldn't do for me to marry until Lizzy has a home of her own, and Jack's learned his trade; for we're not rich, and I must be father to the children and husband to the dear old woman, if I can."

"No doubt but you are both, John; yet how came you to go to war, if you felt so? Wasn't enlisting as bad as marrying?"

"No, ma'am, not as I see it, for one is helping my neighbor, the other pleasing myself. I went because I couldn't help it. I didn't want the glory or the pay; I wanted the right thing done, and people kept saying the men who were in earnest ought to fight. I was in earnest, the Lord knows! but I held off as long as I could, not knowing which was my duty. Mother saw the case, gave me her ring to keep me steady, and said 'Go:' so I went."

A short story and a simple one, but the man and the mother were portrayed better than pages of fine writing could have done it.

"Do you ever regret that you came, when you lie here suffering so much?"

"Never, ma'am; I haven't helped a great deal, but I've shown I was willing to give my life, and perhaps I've got to; but I don't blame anybody, and if it was to do over again, I'd do it. I'm a little sorry I wasn't wounded in front; it looks cowardly to be hit in the back, but I obeyed orders, and it don't matter in the end, I know."

Poor John! it did not matter now, except that a shot in front might have spared the long agony in store for him. He seemed to read the thought that troubled me, as he spoke so hopefully when there was no hope, for he suddenly added:

"This is my first battle; do they think it's going to be my last?"

"I'm afraid they do, John."

It was the hardest question I had ever been called upon to answer; doubly hard with those clear eyes fixed on mine, forcing a truthful answer by their own truth. He seemed a little startled at first, pondered over the fateful fact a moment, then shook his head, with a glance at the broad chest and muscular limbs stretched out before him:

"I'm not afraid, but it's difficult to believe all at once. I'm so strong it don't seem possible for such a little wound to kill me."

Merry Mercutio's dying words glanced through my memory as he spoke: " 'Tis not so deep as a well nor so wide as a church door, but 'tis enough." And John would have said the same could he have seen the ominous black holes between his shoulders; he never had, but, seeing the ghastly sights about him, could not believe his own wound more fatal than these, for all the suffering it caused him.

"Shall I write to your mother, now?" I asked, thinking that these sudden tidings might change all plans and purposes. But they did not; for the man received the order of the Divine Commander to march with the same unquestioning obedience with which the soldier had received that of the human one; doubtless remembering that the first led him to life, and the last to death.

"No, ma'am; to Jack just the same; he'll break it to her best, and I'll add a line to her myself when you get done."

So I wrote the letter which he dictated, finding it better than any I had sent; for, though here and there a little ungrammatical or inelegant, each sentence came to me briefly worded, but most expressive; full of excellent counsel to the boy, tenderly bequeathing "mother and Lizzie" to his care, and bidding him good bye in words the sadder for their simplicity. He added a few lines, with steady hand, and, as I sealed it, said, with a patient sort of sigh, "I hope the answer will come in time for me to see it;" then, turning away his face, laid the flowers against his lips, as if to hide some quiver of emotion at the thought of such a sudden sundering of all the dear home ties.

These things had happened two days before; now John was dying, and the letter had not come. I had been summoned to many death beds in my life, but to none that made my heart ache as it did then, since my mother called me to watch the departure of a spirit akin to this in its gentleness and patient strength. As I went in, John stretched out both hands:

"I knew you'd come! I guess I'm moving on, ma'am."

He was; and so rapidly that, even while he spoke, over his face I saw the grey veil falling that no human hand can lift. I sat down by him, wiped the drops from his forehead, stirred the air about him with the slow wave of a fan, and waited to help him die. He stood in sore need of help—and I could do so little; for, as the doctor had foretold, the strong body rebelled against death, and fought every inch of the way, forcing him to draw each breath with a spasm, and clench his hands with an imploring look, as if he asked, "How long must I endure this, and be still!" For hours he suffered dumbly, without a moment's respite, or a moment's murmuring; his limbs grew cold, his face damp, his lips white, and, again and again, he tore the covering off his breast, as if the lightest weight added to his agony; yet through it all, his eyes never lost their perfect serenity, and the man's soul seemed to sit therein, undaunted by the ills that vexed his flesh.

One by one, the men woke, and round the room appeared a circle of pale faces and watchful eyes, full of awe and pity; for, though a stranger, John was beloved by all. Each man there had wondered at his patience, respected his piety, admired his fortitude, and now lamented his hard death; for the influence of an upright nature had made itself deeply felt, even in one little week. Presently, the Jonathan who so loved this comely David, came creeping from his bed for a last look and word. The kind soul was full of trouble, as the choke in his voice, the grasp of his hand, betrayed; but there were no tears, and the farewell of the friends was the more touching for its brevity.

"Old boy, how are you?" faltered the one.

"Most through, thank heaven!" whispered the other.

"Can I say or do anything for you anywheres?"

"Take my things home, and tell them that I did my best."

"I will! I will!"

"Good bye, Ned."

"Good bye, John, good bye!"

They kissed each other, tenderly as women, and so parted, for poor Ned could not stay to see his comrade die. For a little while, there was no sound in the room but the drip of water, from a stump or two, and John's distressful gasps, as he slowly breathed his life away. I thought him nearly gone, and had just laid down the fan, believing its help to be no longer needed, when suddenly he rose up in his bed, and cried out with a bitter cry that broke the silence, sharply startling every one with its agonized appeal:

"For God's sake, give me air!"

It was the only cry pain or death had wrung from him, the only boon he had asked; and none of us could grant it, for all the airs that blew were useless now. Dan flung up the window. The first red streak of dawn was warming the grey east, a herald of the coming sun; John saw it, and with the love of light which lingers in us to the end, seemed to read in it a sign of hope of help, for, over his whole face there broke that mysterious expression, brighter than any smile, which often comes to eyes that look their last. He laid himself gently down; and, stretching out his strong right arm, as if to grasp and bring the blessed air to his lips in a fuller flow, lapsed into a merciful unconsciousness, which assured us that for him suffering was forever past. He died then; for, though the heavy breaths still tore their way up for a little longer, they were but the waves of an ebbing tide that beat unfelt against the wreck, which an immortal voyager had deserted with a smile. He never spoke again, but to the end held my hand close, so close that when he was asleep at last, I could not draw it away. Dan helped me, warning me as he did so that it was unsafe for dead and living flesh to lie so long together; but though my hand was strangely cold and stiff, and four white marks remained across its back, even when warmth and color had returned elsewhere, I could not but be glad that, through its touch, the presence of human sympathy, perhaps, had lightened that hard hour.

When they had made him ready for the grave, John lay in state for half an hour, a thing which seldom happened in that busy place; but a universal sentiment of reverence and affection seemed to fill the hearts of all who had known or heard of him; and when the rumor of his death went through the house, always astir, many came to see him, and I felt a tender sort of pride in my lost patient; for he looked a most heroic figure, lying there stately and still as the statue of some young knight asleep upon his tomb. The lovely expression which so often beautifies dead faces, soon replaced the marks of pain, and I longed for those who loved him best to see him when half an hour's acquaintance with Death had made them friends. As we stood looking at him, the ward master handed me a letter, saying it had been forgotten the night before. It was John's letter, come just an hour too late to gladden the eyes that had longed and looked for it so eagerly! but he had it; for, after I had cut some brown locks for his mother, and taken off the ring to send her, telling how well the talisman had done its work, I kissed this good son for her sake, and laid the letter in his hand, still folded as when I drew my own away, feeling that its place was there, and making myself happy with the thought, that, even in his solitary grave in the "Government Lot," he would not be without some token of the love which makes life beautiful and outlives death. Then I left him, glad to have known so genuine a man, and carrying with me an enduring memory of the brave Virginia blacksmith, as he lay serenely waiting for the dawn of that long day which knows no night.

My Contraband

DOCTOR FRANCK CAME in as I sat sewing up the rents in an old shirt, that Tom might go tidily to his grave. New shirts were needed for the living, and there was no wife or mother to "dress him handsome when he went to meet the Lord," as one woman said, describing the fine funeral she had pinched herself to give her son.

"Miss Dane, I'm in a quandary," began the Doctor, with that expression of countenance which says as plainly as words, "I want to ask a favor, but I wish you'd save me the trouble."

"Can I help you out of it?"

"Faith! I don't like to propose it, but you certainly can, if you please."

"Then name it, I beg."

"You see a Reb has just been brought in crazy with typhoid; a bad case every way; a drunken, rascally little captain somebody took the trouble to capture, but whom nobody wants to take the trouble to cure. The wards are full, the ladies worked to death, and willing to be for our own boys, but rather slow to risk their lives for a Reb. Now, you've had the fever, you like queer patients, your mate will see to your ward for a while, and I will find you a good attendant. The fellow won't last long, I fancy; but he can't die without some sort of care, you know. I've put him in the fourth story of the west wing, away from the rest. It is airy, quiet, and comfortable there. I'm on that ward, and will do my best for you in every way. Now, then, will you go?"

"Of course I will, out of perversity, if not common charity; for some of these people think that because I'm an abolitionist I am also a heathen, and I should rather like to show them that, though I cannot quite love my enemies, I am willing to take care of them."

"Very good; I thought you'd go; and speaking of abolition reminds me that you can have a contraband for servant, if you like. It is that fine mulatto fellow who was found burying his rebel master after the fight, and, being badly cut over the head, our boys brought him along. Will you have him?"

"By all means,—for I'll stand to my guns on that point, as on the other; these black boys are far more faithful and handy than some of the white scamps given me to serve, instead of being served by. But is this man well enough?"

"Yes, for that sort of work, and I think you'll like him. He must have been a handsome fellow before he got his face slashed; not much darker than myself; his master's son, I dare say, and the white blood makes him rather high and haughty about some things. He was in a bad way when he came in, but vowed he'd die in the street rather than turn in with the black fellows below; so I put him up in the west wing, to be out of the way, and he's seen to the captain all the morning. When can you go up?"

"As soon as Tom is laid out, Skinner moved, Haywood washed, Marble dressed, Charley rubbed, Downs taken up, Upham laid down, and the whole forty fed."

We both laughed, though the Doctor was on his way to the dead-house and I held a shroud on my lap. But in a hospital one learns that cheerfulness is one's salvation; for, in an atmosphere of suffering and death, heaviness of heart would soon paralyze usefulness of hand, if the blessed gift of smiles had been denied us.

In an hour I took possession of my new charge, finding a dissipated-looking boy of nineteen or twenty raving in the solitary little room, with no one near him but the contraband in the room adjoining. Feeling decidedly more interest in the black man than in the white, yet remembering the Doctor's hint of his being "high and haughty," I glanced furtively at him as I scattered chloride of lime about the room to purify the air, and settled matters to suit myself. I had seen many contrabands, but never one so attractive as this. All colored men are called "boys," even if their heads are white; this boy was five-and-twenty at least, strong-limbed and manly, and had the look of one who never had been cowed by abuse or worn with oppressive labor. He sat on his bed doing nothing; no book, no pipe, no pen or paper anywhere appeared, yet anything less indolent or listless than his attitude and expression I never saw. Erect he sat, with a hand on either knee, and eyes fixed on the bare wall opposite, so rapt in some absorbing thought as to be unconscious of my presence, though the door stood wide open and my movements were by no means noiseless. His face was half averted, but I instantly approved the Doctor's taste, for the profile which I saw possessed all the attributes of comeliness belonging to his mixed race. He was more quadroon than mulatto, with Saxon features, Spanish complexion darkened by exposure, color in lips and cheek, waving hair, and an eye full of the passionate melancholy which in such men always seems to utter a mute protest against the broken law that doomed them at their birth. What could he be thinking of? The sick boy cursed and raved, I rustled to and fro, steps passed the door, bells rang, and the steady rumble of army-wagons came up from the street, still he never stirred. I had seen colored people in what they call "the black sulks," when, for days, they neither smiled nor spoke, and scarcely ate. But this was something more than that; for the man was not dully brooding over some small grievance; he seemed to see an all-absorbing fact or fancy recorded on the wall, which was a blank to me. I wondered if it were some deep wrong or sorrow, kept alive by memory and impotent regret; if he mourned for the dead master to whom he had been faithful to the end; or if the liberty now his were robbed of half its sweetness by the knowledge that some one near and dear to him still languished in the hell from which he had escaped. My heart quite warmed to him at that idea; I wanted to know and comfort him; and, following the impulse of the moment, I went in and touched him on the shoulder.

In an instant the man vanished and the slave appeared. Freedom was too new a boon to have wrought its blessed changes yet; and as he started up, with his hand at his temple, and an obsequious "Yes, Missis," any romance that had gathered round him fled away, leaving the saddest of all sad facts in living guise before me. Not only did the manhood seem to die out of him, but the comeliness that first attracted me; for, as he turned, I saw the ghastly wound that had laid open cheek and forehead. Being partly healed, it was no longer bandaged, but held together with strips of that transparent plaster which I never see without a shiver, and swift recollections of the scenes with which it is associated in my mind. Part of his black hair had been shorn away, and one eye was nearly closed; pain so distorted, and the cruel sabre-cut so marred that portion of his face, that, when I saw it, I felt as if a fine medal had been suddenly reversed, showing me a far more striking type of human suffering and wrong than Michael Angelo's bronze prisoner. By one of those inexplicable processes that often teach us how little we understand ourselves, my purpose was suddenly changed; and, though I went in to offer comfort as a friend, I merely gave an order as a mistress.

"Will you open these windows? this man needs more air."

He obeyed at once, and, as he slowly urged up the unruly sash, the handsome profile was again turned toward me, and again I was possessed by my first impression so strongly that I involuntarily said,—

"Thank you."

Perhaps it was fancy, but I thought that in the look of mingled surprise and something like reproach which he gave me, there was also a trace of grateful pleasure. But he said, in that tone of spiritless humility these poor souls learn so soon,—

"I isn't a white man, Missis, I'se a contraband."

"Yes, I know it; but a contraband is a free man, and I heartily congratulate you."

He liked that; his face shone, he squared his shoulders, lifted his head, and looked me full in the eye with a brisk,—

"Thank ye, Missis; anything more to do fer yer?"

"Doctor Franck thought you would help me with this man, as there are many patients and few nurses or attendants. Have you had the fever?"

"No, Missis."

"They should have thought of that when they put him here; wounds and fevers should not be together. I'll try to get you moved."

He laughed a sudden laugh: if he had been a white man, I should have called it scornful; as he was a few shades darker than myself, I suppose it must be considered an insolent, or at least an unmannerly one.

"It don't matter, Missis. I'd rather be up here with the fever than down with those niggers; and there isn't no other place fer me."

Poor fellow! that was true. No ward in all the hospital would take him in to lie side by side with the most miserable white wreck there. Like the bat in Æsop's fable, he belonged to neither race; and the pride of one and the helplessness of the other, kept him hovering alone in the twilight a great sin has brought to overshadow the whole land.

"You shall stay, then; for I would far rather have you than my lazy Jack. But are you well and strong enough?"

"I guess I'll do, Missis."

He spoke with a passive sort of acquiescence,—as if it did not much matter if he were not able, and no one would particularly rejoice if he were.

"Yes, I think you will. By what name shall I call you?"

"Bob, Missis."

Every woman has her pet whim; one of mine was to teach the men self-respect by treating them respectfully. Tom, Dick, and Harry would pass, when lads rejoiced in those familiar abbreviations; but to address men often old enough to be my father in that style did not suit my old-fashioned ideas of propriety. This "Bob" would never do; I should have found it as easy to call the chaplain "Gus" as my tragical-looking contraband by a title so strongly associated with the tail of a kite.

"What is your other name?" I asked. "I like to call my attendants by their last names rather than by their first."

"I'se got no other, Missis; we has our masters' names, or do without. Mine's dead, and I won't have anything of his 'bout me."

"Well, I'll call you Robert, then, and you may fill this pitcher for me, if you will be so kind."

He went; but, through all the tame obedience years of servitude had taught him, I could see that the proud spirit his father gave him was not yet subdued, for the look and gesture with which he repudiated his master's name were a more effective declaration of independence than any Fourth-of-July orator could have prepared.

We spent a curious week together. Robert seldom left his room, except upon my errands; and I was a prisoner all day, often all night, by the bedside of the rebel. The fever burned itself rapidly away, for there seemed little vitality to feed it in the feeble frame of this old young man, whose life had been none of the most righteous, judging from the revelations made by his unconscious lips; since more than once Robert authoritatively silenced him, when my gentler hushings were of no avail, and blasphemous wanderings or ribald camp-songs made my cheeks burn and Robert's face assume an aspect of disgust. The captain was a gentleman in the world's eye, but the contraband was the gentleman in mine;—I was a fanatic, and that accounts for such depravity of taste, I hope. I never asked Robert of himself, feeling that somewhere there was a spot still too sore to bear the lightest touch; but, from his language, manner, and intelligence, I inferred that his color had procured for him the few advantages within the reach of a quick-witted, kindly-treated slave. Silent, grave, and thoughtful, but most serviceable, was my contraband; glad of the books I brought him, faithful in the performance of the duties I assigned to him, grateful for the friendliness I could not but feel and show toward him. Often I longed to ask what purpose was so visibly altering his aspect with such daily deepening gloom. But I never dared, and no one else had either time or desire to pry into the past of this specimen of one branch of the chivalrous "F.F.Vs."[1]

On the seventh night, Dr. Franck suggested that it would be well for some one, besides the general watchman of the ward, to be with the captain, as it might be his last. Although the greater part of the two preceding nights had been spent there, of course I offered to remain,—for there is a strange fascination in these scenes, which renders one careless of fatigue and unconscious of fear until the crisis is past.

"Give him water as long as he can drink, and if he drops into a natural sleep, it may save him. I'll look in at midnight, when some change will

1. *"F. F. Vs."*] First Families of Virginia, i.e., the socially elite families.

probably take place. Nothing but sleep or a miracle will keep him now. Good-night."

Away went the Doctor; and, devouring a whole mouthful of grapes, I lowered the lamp, wet the captain's head, and sat down on a hard stool to begin my watch. The captain lay with his hot, haggard face turned toward me, filling the air with his poisonous breath, and feebly muttering, with lips and tongue so parched that the sanest speech would have been difficult to understand. Robert was stretched on his bed in the inner room, the door of which stood ajar, that a fresh draught from his open window might carry the fever-fumes away through mine. I could just see a long, dark figure, with the lighter outline of a face, and, having little else to do just then, I fell to thinking of this curious contraband, who evidently prized his freedom highly, yet seemed in no haste to enjoy it. Dr. Franck had offered to send him on to safer quarters, but he had said, "No, thank yer, sir, not yet," and then had gone away to fall into one of those black moods of his, which began to disturb me, because I had no power to lighten them. As I sat listening to the clocks from the steeples all about us, I amused myself with planning Robert's future, as I often did my own, and had dealt out to him a generous hand of trumps wherewith to play this game of life which hitherto had gone so cruelly against him, when a harsh choked voice called,—

"Lucy!"

It was the captain, and some new terror seemed to have gifted him with momentary strength.

"Yes, here's Lucy," I answered, hoping that by following the fancy I might quiet him,—for his face was damp with the clammy moisture, and his frame shaken with the nervous tremor that so often precedes death. His dull eye fixed upon me, dilating with a bewildered look of incredulity and wrath, till he broke out fiercely,—

"That's a lie! she's dead,—and so's Bob, damn him!"

Finding speech a failure, I began to sing the quiet tune that had often soothed delirium like this; but hardly had the line,—

"See gentle patience smile on pain,"

passed my lips, when he clutched me by the wrist, whispering like one in mortal fear,—

"Hush! she used to sing that way to Bob, but she never would to me. I swore I'd whip the devil out of her, and I did; but you know before she cut her throat she said she'd haunt me, and there she is!"

He pointed behind me with an aspect of such pale dismay, that I involuntarily glanced over my shoulder and started as if I had seen a veritable ghost; for, peering from the gloom of that inner room, I saw a shadowy face, with dark hair all about it, and a glimpse of scarlet at the throat. An instant showed me that it was only Robert leaning from his bed's foot, wrapped in a gray army-blanket, with his red shirt just visible above it, and his long hair disordered by sleep. But what a strange expression was on his face! The unmarred side was toward me, fixed and motionless as when I first observed it,—less absorbed now, but more intent. His eye glittered, his lips were apart like one who listened with every sense, and his whole aspect reminded me of a hound to which some wind had brought the scent of unsuspected prey.

"Do you know him, Robert? Does he mean you?"

"Laws, no, Missis; they all own half-a-dozen Bobs: but hearin' my name woke me; that's all."

He spoke quite naturally, and lay down again, while I returned to my charge, thinking that this paroxysm was probably his last. But by another hour I perceived a hopeful change; for the tremor had subsided, the cold dew was gone, his breathing was more regular, and Sleep, the healer, had descended to save or take him gently away. Doctor Franck looked in at midnight, bade me keep all cool and quiet, and not fail to administer a certain draught as soon as the captain woke. Very much relieved, I laid my head on my arms, uncomfortably folded on the little table, and fancied I was about to perform one of the feats which practice renders possible,—"sleeping with one eye open," as we say: a half-and-half doze, for all senses sleep but that of hearing; the faintest murmur, sigh, or motion will break it, and give one back one's wits much brightened by the brief permission to "stand at ease." On this night the experiment was a failure, for previous vigils, confinement, and much care had rendered naps a dangerous indulgence. Having roused half-a-dozen times in an hour to find all quiet, I dropped my heavy head on my arms, and, drowsily resolving to look up again in fifteen minutes, fell fast asleep.

The striking of a deep-voiced clock awoke me with a start. "That is one," thought I; but, to my dismay, two more strokes followed, and in remorseful haste I sprang up to see what harm my long oblivion had done. A strong hand put me back into my seat, and held me there. It was Robert. The instant my eye met his my heart began to beat, and all along my nerves tingled that electric flash which foretells a danger that we cannot see. He was very pale, his mouth grim, and both eyes full of sombre fire; for even the wounded one was open now, all the more sinister for the deep scar above and below. But his touch was steady, his voice quiet, as he said,—

"Sit still, Missis; I won't hurt yer, nor scare yer, ef I can help it, but yer waked too soon."

"Let me go, Robert,—the captain is stirring,—I must give him something."

"No, Missis, yer can't stir an inch. Look here!"

Holding me with one hand, with the other he took up the glass in which I had left the draught, and showed me it was empty.

"Has he taken it?" I asked, more and more bewildered.

"I flung it out o' winder, Missis; he'll have to do without."

"But why, Robert? why did you do it?"

" 'Kase I hate him!"

Impossible to doubt the truth of that; his whole face showed it, as he spoke through his set teeth, and launched a fiery glance at the unconscious captain. I could only hold my breath and stare blankly at him, wondering what mad act was coming next. I suppose I shook and turned white, as women have a foolish habit of doing when sudden danger daunts them; for Robert released my arm, sat down upon the bedside just in front of me, and said, with the ominous quietude that made me cold to see and hear,—

"Don't yer be frightened, Missis; don't try to run away, fer the door's locked and the key in my pocket; don't yer cry out, fer yer'd have to scream a long while, with my hand on yer mouth, 'efore yer was heard. Be still, an' I'll tell yer what I'm gwine to do."

"Lord help us! he has taken the fever in some sudden, violent way, and is out of his head. I must humor him till some one comes"; in pursuance of which swift determination, I tried to say, quite composedly,—

"I will be still and hear you; but open the window. Why did you shut it?"

"I'm sorry I can't do it, Missis; but yer'd jump out, or call, if I did, an' I'm not ready yet. I shut it to make yer sleep, an' heat would do it quicker'n anything else I could do."

The captain moved, and feebly muttered "Water!" Instinctively I rose to give it to him, but the heavy hand came down upon my shoulder, and in the same decided tone Robert said,—

"The water went with the physic; let him call."

"Do let me go to him! he'll die without care!"

"I mean he shall;—don't yer meddle, if yer please, Missis."

In spite of his quiet tone and respectful manner, I saw murder in his eyes, and turned faint with fear; yet the fear excited me, and, hardly knowing what I did, I seized the hands that had seized me, crying,—

"No, no; you shall not kill him! It is base to hurt a helpless man. Why do you hate him? He is not your master."

"He's my brother."

I felt that answer from head to foot, and seemed to fathom what was coming, with a prescience vague, but unmistakable. One appeal was left to me, and I made it.

"Robert, tell me what it means? Do not commit a crime and make me accessory to it. There is a better way of righting wrong than by violence;—let me help you find it."

My voice trembled as I spoke, and I heard the frightened flutter of my heart; so did he, and if any little act of mine had ever won affection or respect from him, the memory of it served me then. He looked down, and seemed to put some question to himself; whatever it was, the answer was in my favor, for when his eyes rose again, they were gloomy, but not desperate.

"I *will* tell yer, Missis; but mind, this makes no difference; the boy is mine. I'll give the Lord a chance to take him fust: if He don't, I shall."

"Oh, no! remember he is your brother."

An unwise speech; I felt it as it passed my lips, for a black frown gathered on Robert's face, and his strong hands closed with an ugly sort of grip. But he did not touch the poor soul gasping there behind him, and seemed content to let the slow suffocation of that stifling room end his frail life.

"I'm not like to forgit dat, Missis, when I've been thinkin' of it all this week. I knew him when they fetched him in, an' would 'a'done it long 'fore this, but I wanted to ask where Lucy was; he knows,—he told to-night,—an' now he's done for."

"Who is Lucy?" I asked hurriedly, intent on keeping his mind busy with any thought but murder.

With one of the swift transitions of a mixed temperament like this, at my question Robert's deep eyes filled, the clenched hands were spread before his face, and all I heard were the broken words,—

"My wife,—he took her——"

In that instant every thought of fear was swallowed up in burning indignation for the wrong, and a perfect passion of pity for the desperate man so tempted to avenge an injury for which there seemed no redress but this. He was no longer slave or contraband, no drop of black blood marred him in my sight, but an infinite compassion yearned to save, to help, to comfort him. Words seemed so powerless I offered none, only put my hand on his poor head, wounded, homeless, bowed down with grief for which I had no cure, and softly smoothed the long, neglected hair, pitifully wondering the while where was the wife who must have loved this tender-hearted man so well.

The captain moaned again, and faintly whispered, "Air!" but I never stirred. God forgive me! just then I hated him as only a woman thinking of a sister woman's wrong could hate. Robert looked up; his eyes were dry again, his mouth grim. I saw that, said, "Tell me more," and he did; for sympathy is a gift the poorest may give, the proudest stoop to receive.

"Yer see, Missis, his father,—I might say ours, ef I warn't ashamed of both of 'em,—his father died two years ago, an' left us all to Marster Ned,—that's him here, eighteen then. He always hated me, I looked so like old Marster: he don't,—only the light skin an' hair. Old Marster was kind to all of us, me 'specially, an' bought Lucy off the next plantation down there in South Car'lina, when he found I liked her. I married her, all I could; it warn't much, but we was true to one another till Marster Ned come home a year after an' made hell fer both of us. He sent my old mother to be used up in his rice-swamp in Georgy; he found me with my pretty Lucy, an' though young Miss cried, an' I prayed to him on my knees, an' Lucy run away, he wouldn't have no mercy; he brought her back, an'—took her."

"Oh, what did you do?" I cried, hot with helpless pain and passion.

How the man's outraged heart sent the blood flaming up into his face and deepened the tones of his impetuous voice, as he stretched his arm across the bed, saying, with a terribly expressive gesture,—

"I half murdered him, an' to-night I'll finish."

"Yes, yes,—but go on now; what came next?"

He gave me a look that showed no white man could have felt a deeper degradation in remembering and confessing these last acts of brotherly oppression.

"They whipped me till I couldn't stand, an' then they sold me further South. Yer thought I was a white man once,—look here!"

With a sudden wrench he tore the shirt from neck to waist, and on his strong, brown shoulders showed me furrows deeply ploughed, wounds which, though healed, were ghastlier to me than any in that house. I could not speak to him, and, with the pathetic dignity a great grief lends the humblest sufferer, he ended his brief tragedy by simply saying,—

"That's all, Missis. I'se never seen her since, an' now I never shall in this world,—maybe not in t'other."

"But, Robert, why think her dead? The captain was wandering when he said those sad things; perhaps he will retract them when he is sane. Don't despair; don't give up yet."

"No, Missis, I 'spect he's right; she was too proud to bear that long. It's like her to kill herself. I told her to, if there was no other way; an' she always minded me, Lucy did. My poor girl! Oh, it warn't right! No, by God, it warn't!"

As the memory of this bitter wrong, this double bereavement, burned in his sore heart, the devil that lurks in every strong man's blood leaped up; he put his hand upon his brother's throat, and, watching the white face before him, muttered low between his teeth,—

"I'm lettin' him go too easy; there's no pain in this; we a'n't even yet. I wish he knew me. Marster Ned! it's Bob; where's Lucy?"

From the captain's lips there came a long faint sigh, and nothing but a flutter of the eyelids showed that he still lived. A strange stillness filled the room as the elder brother held the younger's life suspended in his hand, while wavering between a dim hope and a deadly hate. In the whirl of thoughts that went on in my brain, only one was clear enough to act upon. I must prevent murder, if I could,—but how? What could I do up there alone, locked in with a dying man and a lunatic?—for any mind yielded utterly to any unrighteous impulse is mad while the impulse rules it. Strength I had not, nor much courage, neither time nor wit for stratagem, and chance only could bring me help before it was too late. But one weapon I possessed,—a tongue,—often a woman's best defence; and sympathy, stronger than fear, gave me power to use it. What I said Heaven only knows, but surely Heaven helped me; words burned on my lips, tears streamed from my eyes, and some good angel prompted me to use the one name that had power to arrest my hearer's hand and touch his heart. For at that moment I heartily believed that Lucy lived, and this earnest faith roused in him a like belief.

He listened with the lowering look of one in whom brute instinct was sovereign for the time,—a look that makes the noblest countenance base. He was but a man,—a poor, untaught, outcast, outraged man. Life had few joys for him; the world offered him no honors, no success, no home, no love. What future would this crime mar? and why should he deny himself that sweet, yet bitter morsel called revenge? How many white men, with all New England's freedom, culture, Christianity, would not have felt as he felt then? Should I have reproached him for a human anguish, a human longing for redress, all now left him from the ruin of his few poor hopes? Who had taught him that self-control, self-sacrifice, are attributes that make men masters of the earth, and lift them nearer heaven? Should I have urged the beauty of forgiveness, the duty of devout submission? He had no religion, for he was no saintly "Uncle Tom," and Slavery's black shadow seemed to darken all the world to him, and shut out God. Should I have warned him of penalties, of judgments, and the poteney of law? What did he know of justice, or the mercy that should temper that stern virtue, when every law, human and divine, had been broken on his hearthstone? Should I have tried to touch him by appeals to filial duty, to brotherly love? How had his appeals been answered? What memories had father and brother stored up in his heart to plead for either now? No,—all these influences, these associations, would have proved worse than useless, had I been calm enough to try them. I was not; but instinct, subtler than reason, showed me the one safe clue by which to lead this troubled soul from the labyrinth in which it groped and nearly fell. When I paused, breathless, Robert turned to me, asking, as if human assurances could strengthen his faith in Divine Omnipotence,—

"Do you believe, if I let Marster Ned live, the Lord will give me back my Lucy?"

"As surely as there is a Lord, you will find her here or in the beautiful hereafter, where there is no black or white, no master and no slave."

He took his hand from his brother's throat, lifted his eyes from my face to the wintry sky beyond, as if searching for that blessed country, happier even than the happy North. Alas, it was the darkest hour before the dawn!—there was no star above, no light below but the pale glimmer of the lamp that showed the brother who had made him desolate. Like a blind man who believes there is a sun, yet cannot see it, he shook his head, let his arms drop nervelessly upon his knees, and sat there dumbly asking that question which many a soul whose faith is firmer fixed than his has asked in hours less dark than this,—"Where is God?" I saw the tide had turned, and strenuously tried to keep this rudderless life-boat from slipping back into the whirlpool wherein it had been so nearly lost.

"I have listened to you, Robert; now hear me, and heed what I say, because my heart is full of pity for you, full of hope for your future, and a desire to help you now. I want you to go away from here, from the temptation of this place, and the sad thoughts that haunt it. You have conquered yourself once, and I honor you for it, because, the harder the battle, the more glorious the victory; but it is safer to put a greater distance between you and this man. I will write you letters, give you money, and send you to good old Massachusetts to begin your new life a freeman,—yes, and a happy man; for when the captain is himself again, I will learn where Lucy is, and move heaven and earth to find and give her back to you. Will you do this, Robert?"

Slowly, very slowly, the answer came; for the purpose of a week, perhaps a year, was hard to relinquish in an hour.

"Yes, Missis, I will."

"Good! Now you are the man I thought you, and I'll work for you with all my heart. You need sleep, my poor fellow; go, and try to forget. The captain is alive, and as yet you are spared that sin. No, don't look there; I'll care for him. Come, Robert, for Lucy's sake."

Thank Heaven for the immortality of love! for when all other means of salvation failed, a spark of this vital fire softened the man's iron will, until a woman's hand could bend it. He let me take from him the key, let me draw him gently away, and lead him to the solitude which now was the most healing balm I could bestow. Once in his little room, he fell down on his bed and lay there, as if spent with the sharpest conflict of his life. I slipped the bolt across his door, and unlocked my own, flung up the window, steadied myself with a breath of air, then rushed to Doctor Franck. He came; and till dawn we worked together, saving one brother's life, and taking earnest thought how best to secure the other's liberty. When the sun came up as blithely as if it shone only upon happy homes, the Doctor went to Robert. For an hour I heard the murmur of their voices; once I caught the sound of heavy sobs, and for a time a reverent hush, as if in the silence that good man were ministering to soul as well as body. When he departed he took Robert with him, pausing to tell me he should get him off as soon as possible, but not before we met again.

Nothing more was seen of them all day; another surgeon came to see the captain, and another attendant came to fill the empty place. I tried to rest, but could not, with the thought of poor Lucy tugging at my heart, and was soon back at my post again, anxiously hoping that my contraband had not been too hastily spirited away. Just as night fell there came a tap, and, opening, I saw Robert literally "clothed, and in his right mind." The Doctor had replaced the ragged suit with tidy garments, and no trace of that tempestuous night remained but deeper lines upon the forehead, and the docile look of a repentant child. He did not cross the threshold, did not offer me his hand,—only took off his cap, saying, with a traitorous falter in his voice,—

"God bless yer, Missis! I'm gwine."

I put out both my hands, and held his fast.

"Good-by, Robert! Keep up good heart, and when I come home to Massachusetts we'll meet in a happier place than this. Are you quite ready, quite comfortable for your journey?"

"Yes, Missis, yes; the Doctor's fixed everything; I'se gwine with a friend of his; my papers are all right, an' I'm as happy as I can be till I find"——

He stopped there; then went on, with a glance into the room,—

"I'm glad I didn't do it, an' I thank yer, Missis, fer hinderin' me,—thank yer hearty; but I'm afraid I hate him jest the same."

Of course he did; and so did I; for these faulty hearts of ours cannot turn perfect in a night, but need frost and fire, wind and rain, to ripen and make them ready for the great harvest-home. Wishing to divert his mind, I put my poor mite into his hand, and, remembering the magic of a certain little book, I gave him mine, on whose dark cover whitely shone the Virgin Mother and the Child, the grand history of whose life the book contained. The money went into Robert's pocket with a grateful murmur, the book into his bosom, with a long look and a tremulous—

"I never saw *my* baby, Missis."

I broke down then; and though my eyes were too dim to see, I felt the touch of lips upon my hands, heard the sound of departing feet, and knew my contraband was gone.

When one feels an intense dislike, the less one says about the subject of it the better; therefore I shall merely record that the captain lived,—in time was exchanged; and that, whoever the other party was, I am convinced the Government got the best of the bargain. But long before this occurred, I had fulfilled my promise to Robert; for as soon as my patient recovered strength of memory enough to make his answer trustworthy, I asked, without any circumlocution,—

"Captain Fairfax, where is Lucy?"

And too feeble to be angry, surprised, or insincere, he straightway answered,—

"Dead, Miss Dane."

"And she killed herself when you sold Bob?"

"How the devil did you know that?" he muttered, with an expression half-remorseful, half-amazed; but I was satisfied, and said no more.

Of course this went to Robert, waiting far away there in a lonely home,—waiting, working, hoping for his Lucy. It almost broke my heart to do it; but delay was weak, deceit was wicked; so I sent the heavy tidings, and very soon the answer came,—only three lines; but I felt that the sustaining power of the man's life was gone.

"I tort I'd never see her any more; I'm glad to know she's out of trouble. I thank yer, Missis; an' if they let us, I'll fight fer yer till I'm killed, which I hope will be 'fore long."

Six months later he had his wish, and kept his word.

Every one knows the story of the attack on Fort Wagner; but we should not tire yet of recalling how our Fifty-Fourth, spent with three sleepless nights, a day's fast, and a march under the July sun, stormed the fort as night fell, facing death in many shapes, following their brave leaders through a fiery rain of shot and shell, fighting valiantly for "God and Governor Andrew,"—how the regiment that went into action seven hundred strong, came out having had nearly half its number captured, killed, or wounded, leaving their young commander to be buried, like a chief of earlier times, with his body-guard around him, faithful to the death. Surely, the insult turns to honor, and the wide grave needs no monument but the heroism that consecrates it in our sight; surely, the hearts that held him nearest, see through their tears a noble victory in the seeming sad defeat; and surely, God's benediction was bestowed, when this loyal soul answered, as Death called the roll, "Lord, here am I, with the brothers Thou hast given me!"

The future must show how well that fight was fought; for though Fort Wagner once defied us, public prejudice is down; and through the cannon-smoke of that black night, the manhood of the colored race shines before many eyes that would not see, rings in many ears that would not hear, wins many hearts that would not hitherto believe.

When the news came that we were needed, there was none so glad as I to leave teaching contrabands, the new work I had taken up, and go to nurse "our boys," as my dusky flock so proudly called the wounded of the Fifty-Fourth. Feeling more satisfaction, as I assumed my big apron and turned up my cuffs, than if dressing for the President's levee, I fell to work in Hospital No. 10 at Beaufort. The scene was most familiar, and yet strange; for only dark faces looked up at me from the pallets so thickly laid along the floor, and I missed the sharp accent of my Yankee boys in the slower, softer voices calling cheerily to one another, or answering my questions with a stout, "We'll never give it up, Missis, till the last Reb's dead," or, "If our people's free, we can afford to die."

Passing from bed to bed, intent on making one pair of hands do the work of three, at least, I gradually washed, fed, and bandaged my way down the long line of sable heroes, and coming to the very last, found that he was my contraband. So old, so worn, so deathly weak and wan, I never should have known him but for the deep scar on his cheek. That side lay uppermost, and caught my eye at once; but even then I doubted, such an awful change had come upon him, when, turning to the ticket just above his head, I saw the name, "Robert Dane." That both assured and touched me, for, remembering that he had no name, I knew that he had taken mine. I longed for him to speak to me, to tell how he had fared since I lost sight of him, and let me perform some little service for him in return for many he had done for me; but he seemed asleep; and as I stood re-living that strange night again, a bright lad, who lay next him softly waving an old fan across both beds, looked up and said,—

"I guess you know him, Missis?"

"You are right. Do you?"

"As much as any one was able to, Missis."

"Why do you say 'was,' as if the man were dead and gone?"

"I s'pose because I know he'll have to go. He's got a bad jab in the breast, an' is bleedin' inside, the Doctor says. He don't suffer any, only gets weaker 'n' weaker every minute. I've been fannin' him this long while, an' he's talked a little; but he don't know me now, so he's most gone, I guess."

There was so much sorrow and affection in the boy's face, that I remembered something, and asked, with redoubled interest,—

"Are you the one that brought him off? I was told about a boy who nearly lost his life in saving that of his mate."

I dare say the young fellow blushed, as any modest lad might have done; I could not see it, but I heard the chuckle of satisfaction that escaped him, as he glanced from his shattered arm and bandaged side to the pale figure opposite.

"Lord, Missis, that's nothin'; we boys always stan' by one another, an' I warn't goin' to leave him to be tormented any more by them cussed Rebs. He's been a slave once, though he don't look half so much like it as me, an' I was born in Boston."

He did not; for the speaker was as black as the ace of spades,—being a sturdy specimen, the knave of clubs would perhaps be a fitter representative,—but the dark freeman looked at the white slave with the pitiful, yet puzzled expression I have so often seen on the faces of our wisest men, when this tangled question of Slavery presented itself, asking to be cut or patiently undone.

"Tell me what you know of this man; for, even if he were awake, he is too weak to talk."

"I never saw him till I joined the regiment, an' no one 'peared to have got much out of him. He was a shut-up sort of feller, an' didn't seem to care for anything but gettin' at the Rebs. Some say he was the fust man of us that enlisted; I know he fretted till we were off, an' when we pitched into old Wagner, he fought like the devil."

"Were you with him when he was wounded? How was it?"

"Yes, Missis. There was somethin' queer about it; for he 'peared to know the chap that killed him, an' the chap knew him. I don't dare to ask, but I rather guess one owned the other some time; for, when they clinched, the chap sung out, 'Bob!' an' Dane, 'Marster Ned!'—then they went at it."

I saw down suddenly, for the old anger and compassion struggled in my heart, and I both longed and feared to hear what was to follow.

"You see, when the Colonel,—Lord keep an' send him back to

us!—it a'n't certain yet, you know, Missis, though it's two days ago we lost him,—well, when the Colonel shouted, 'Rush on, boys, rush on!' Dane tore away as if he was goin' to take the fort alone; I was next him, an' kept close as we went through the ditch an' up the wall. Hi! warn't that a rusher!" and the boy flung up his well arm with a whoop, as if the mere memory of that stirring moment came over him in a gust of irrepressible excitement.

"Were you afraid?" I said, asking the question women often put, and receiving the answer they seldom fail to get.

"No, Missis!"—emphasis on the "Missis"—"I never thought of anything but the damn' Rebs, that scalp, slash, an' cut our ears off, when they git us. I was bound to let daylight into one of 'em at least, an' I did. Hope he liked it!"

"It is evident that you did. Now go on about Robert, for I should be at work."

"He was one of the fust up; I was just behind, an' though the whole thing happened in a minute, I remember how it was, for all I was yellin' an' knockin' round like mad. Just where we were, some sort of an officer was wavin' his sword an' cheerin' on his men; Dane saw him by a big flash that come by; he flung away his gun, give a leap, an' went at that feller as if he was Jeff, Beauregard, an' Lee, all in one. I scrabbled after as quick as I could, but was only up in time to see him git the sword straight through him an' drop into the ditch. You needn't ask what I did next, Missis, for I don't quite know myself; all I'm clear about is, that I managed somehow to pitch that Reb into the fort as dead as Moses, git hold of Dane, an' bring him off. Poor old feller! we said we went in to live or die; he said he went in to die, an' he's done it."

I had been intently watching the excited speaker; but as he regretfully added those last words I turned again, and Robert's eyes met mine,—those melancholy eyes, so full of an intelligence that proved he had heard, remembered, and reflected with that preternatural power which often outlives all other faculties. He knew me, yet gave no greeting; was glad to see a woman's face, yet had no smile wherewith to welcome it; felt that he was dying, yet uttered no farewell. He was too far across the river to return or linger now; departing thought, strength, breath, were spent in one grateful look, one murmur of submission to the last pang he could ever feel. His lips moved, and, bending to them, a whisper chilled my cheek, as it shaped the broken words,—

"I'd 'a' done it,—but it's better so,—I'm satisfied."

Ah! well he might be,—for, as he turned his face from the shadow of the life that was, the sunshine of the life to be touched it with a beautiful content, and in the drawing of a breath my contraband found wife and home, eternal liberty and God.

Happy Women

ONE OF THE trials of woman-kind is the fear of being an old maid. To escape this dreadful doom, young girls rush into matrimony with a recklessness which astonishes the beholder; never pausing to remember that the loss of liberty, happiness, and self-respect is poorly repaid by the barren honor of being called "Mrs." instead of "Miss."

Fortunately, this foolish prejudice is fast disappearing, conquered by the success of a certain class belonging to the sisterhood. This class is composed of superior women who, from various causes, remain single, and devote themselves to some earnest work; espousing philanthropy, art, literature, music, medicine, or whatever task taste, necessity, or chance suggests, and remaining as faithful to and as happy in their choice as married women with husbands and homes. It being my good fortune to know several such, I venture to offer a little sketch of them to those of my young countrywomen who, from choice or necessity, stand along, seeking to find the happiness which is the right of all.

Here is L., a rich man's daughter; pretty, accomplished, sensible, and good. She tried fashionable life and found that it did not satisfy her. No lover was happy enough to make a response in her heart, and at twenty-three she looked about her for something to occupy and interest her. She was attracted towards the study of medicine; became absorbed in it; went alone to Paris and London; studied faithfully; received her diploma, and, having practised successfully for a time, was appointed the resident physician of a city hospital. Here, doing a truly womanly work, she finds no time for ennui, unhappiness, or the vague longing for something to fill heart and life, which leads so many women to take refuge in frivolous or dangerous amusements and pursuits. She never talks of her mission or her rights, but beautifully fulfils the one and quietly assumes the others. Few criticise or condemn her course, and none question her success. Respected and beloved by all who know her, she finds genuine satisfaction in her work, and is the busiest, happiest, most useful woman whom I know.

Next comes M., a brilliant, talented girl, full of energy, ambition, and noble aspirations. Poor, yet attractive, through natural gifts and graces, to her came the great temptation of such a girl's life—a rich lover; an excellent young man, but her inferior in all respects. She felt this, and so did he, but hoping that love would make them equals, he urged his suit.

"If I loved him," she said, "my way would be plain, and I should not hesitate a minute. But I do not; I've tried, and I am sure I *never* can feel toward him as I should. It is a great temptation, for I long to cultivate my talent to help my family, to see the world, and enjoy life, and all this may be done if I said 'Yes.' People tell me that I am foolish to reject this good fortune; that it is my duty to accept it; that I shall get on very well without love, and talk as if it were a business transaction. It is hard to say 'No'; but I *must,* for in marriage I want to look up, not down. I cannot make it seem right to take this offer, and I must let it go, for I dare not sell my liberty."

She made her choice, turned away from the pleasant future laid before her, and took up her load again. With her one talent in her hand she faced poverty, cheerfully teaching music, year after year; hoping always, complaining never, and finding herself a stronger, happier woman for that act: A richer woman also; for, though the husband was lost a true friend was gained—since the lover, with respect added to his love, said manfully, "She is right; God bless her!"

S. is poor, plain, ungifted, and ordinary in all things but one—a cheerful, helpful spirit, that loves its neighbor better than itself, and cannot rest till it has proved its sincerity. Few, so placed, would have lived forty hard, dull years without becoming either sharp and sour, or bitter and blue. But S. is as sweet and sunny as a child; and, to those who know her, the personification of content. The only talent she possesses is that of loving every helpless, suffering, forlorn and outcast creature whom she meets. Finding her round of home duties too small for her benevolence, she became one of the home missionaries, whose reports are never read, whose salaries are never paid of earth. Poverty-stricken homes, sick-beds, sinful souls, and sorrowing hearts attract her as irresistibly as pleasure attracts other women, and she faithfully ministers to such, unknown and unrewarded.

"I never had a lover, and I never can have you know. I'm *so* plain," she says, with a smile that is pathetic in its humility, its unconscious wistfulness.

She is mistaken here; for there are many to whom that plain face is beautiful, that helpful hand very dear. Her lovers are not of the romantic sort; but old women, little children, erring men, and forlorn girls give her an affection as endearing and sincere as any husband could have done. Few will know her worth here, but, in the long hereafter, I am sure S. will be blest with eternal beauty, happiness, and love.

A. is a woman of a strongly individual type, who in the course of an unusually varied experience has seen so much of what a wise man has called "the tragedy of modern married life," that she is afraid to try it. Knowing that for one of a peculiar nature like herself such an experiment would be doubly hazardous, she has obeyed instinct and become a chronic old maid. Filial and fraternal love must satisfy her, and grateful that such ties are possible, she lives for them and is content. Literature is a fond and faithful spouse, and the little family that has sprung up around her, though perhaps unlovely and uninteresting to others, is a profitable source of satisfaction to her maternal heart. After a somewhat tempestuous voyage, she is glad to find herself in a quiet haven whence she can look back upon her vanished youth and feel that though the blossom time of life is past, a little fruit remains to ripen in the early autumn coming on. Not lonely, for parents, brothers and sisters, friends and babies keep her heart full and warm; not idle, for necessity, stern, yet kindly teacher, has taught her the worth of work; not unhappy, for love and labor, like good angels, walk at either hand, and the divine Friend fills the world with strength and beauty for the soul and eyes that have learned to see it thankfully.

My sisters, don't be afraid of the words, "old maid," for it is in your power to make this a term of honor, not reproach. It is not necessary to be a sour, spiteful spinster, with nothing to do but brew tea, talk scandal and tend a pocket-handkerchief. No, the world is full of work, needing all the heads, hearts, and hands we can bring to do it. Never was there so splendid an opportunity for women to enjoy their liberty and prove that they deserve it by using it wisely. If love comes as it should come, accept it in God's name and be worthy of His best blessing. If it never comes, then in God's name reject the shadow of it, for that can never satisfy a hungry heart. Do not be ashamed to own the truth—do not be daunted by the fear of ridicule and loneliness, nor saddened by the loss of a woman's tenderest ties. Be true to yourselves; cherish whatever talent you possess, and in using it faithfully for the good of others you will most assuredly find happiness for yourself, and make of life no failure, but a beautiful success.

How I Went Out to Service

WHEN I WAS eighteen I wanted something to do. I had tried teaching for two years, and hated it; I had tried sewing, and could not earn my bread in that way, at the cost of health; I tried story-writing and got five dollars for stories which now bring a hundred; I had thought seriously of going upon the stage, but certain highly respectable relatives were so shocked at the mere idea that I relinquished my dramatic aspirations.

"What *shall* I do?" was still the question that perplexed me. I was ready to work, eager to be independent, and too proud to endure patronage. But the right task seemed hard to find, and my bottled energies were fermenting in a way that threatened an explosion before long.

My honored mother was a city missionary that winter, and not only served the clamorous poor, but often found it in her power to help decayed gentlefolk by quietly placing them where they could earn their bread without the entire sacrifice of taste and talent which makes poverty so hard for such to bear. Knowing her tact and skill, people often came to her for companions, housekeepers, and that class of the needy who do not make their wants known through an intelligence office.

One day, as I sat dreaming splendid dreams, while I made a series of little petticoats out of the odds and ends sent in for the poor, a tall, ministerial gentleman appeared, in search of a companion for his sister. He possessed an impressive nose, a fine flow of language, and a pair of large hands, encased in black kid gloves. With much waving of these somber members, Mr. R. set forth the delights awaiting the happy soul who should secure this home. He described it as a sort of heaven on earth. "There are books, pictures, flowers, a piano, and the best of society," he said. "This person will be one of the family in all respects, and only required to help about the lighter work, which my sister has done herself hitherto, but is now a martyr to neuralgia and needs a gentle friend to assist her."

My mother, who never lost her faith in human nature, in spite of many impostures, believed every word, and quite beamed with benevolent interest as she listened and tried to recall some needy young woman to whom this charming home would be a blessing. I also innocently thought:

"That sounds inviting. I like housework and can do it well. I should have time to enjoy the books and things I love, and D— is not far away from home. Suppose I try it."

So, when my mother turned to me, asking if I could suggest any one, I became as red as a poppy and said abruptly:

"Only myself."

"Do you really mean it?" cried my astonished parent.

"I really do if Mr. R. thinks I should suit," was my steady reply, as I partially obscured my crimson countenance behind a little flannel skirt, still redder.

The Reverend Josephus gazed upon me with the benign regard which a bachelor of five and thirty may accord a bashful damsel of eighteen. A smile dawned upon his countenance, "sicklied o'er with the pale cast of thought," or dyspepsia; and he softly folded the black gloves, as if about to bestow a blessing as he replied, with emphasis:

"I am sure you would, and we should think ourselves most fortunate if we could secure your society, and—ahem—services for my poor sister."

"Then I'll try it," responded the impetuous maid.

"We will talk it over a little first, and let you know to-morrow, sir," put in my prudent parent, adding, as Mr. R. arose: "What wages do you pay?"

"My dear madam, in a case like this let me not use such words as those. Anything you may think proper we shall gladly give. The labor is very light, for there are but three of us and our habits are of the simplest sort. I am a frail reed and may break at any moment; so is my sister, and my aged father cannot long remain; therefore, money is little to us, and any one who comes to lend her youth and strength to our feeble household will not be forgotten in the end, I assure you." And, with another pensive smile, a farewell wave of the impressive gloves, the Reverend Josephus bowed like a well-sweep and departed.

"My dear, are you in earnest?" asked my mother.

"Of course, I am. Why not try this experiment? It can but fail, like all the others."

"I have no objection; only I fancied you were rather too proud for this sort of thing."

"I am too proud to be idle and dependent, ma'am. I'll scrub floors and take in washing first. I do housework at home for love; why not do it abroad for money? I like it better than teaching. It is healthier than sewing and surer than writing. So why not try it?"

"It is going out to service, you know, though you are called a companion. How does that suit?"

"I don't care. Every sort of work that is paid for is service; and I don't mind being a companion, if I can do it well. I may find it is my mission to take care of neuralgic old ladies and lackadaisical clergymen. It does not sound exciting, but it's better than nothing," I answered, with a sigh; for it *was* rather a sudden downfall to give up being a Siddons and become a Betcinder.

How my sisters laughed when they heard the new plan! But they soon resigned themselves, sure of fun, for Lu's adventures were the standing joke of the family. Of course, the highly respectable relatives held up their hands in holy horror at the idea of one of the clan degrading herself by going out to service. Teaching a private school was the proper thing for an indigent gentlewoman. Sewing even, if done in the seclusion of home and not mentioned in public, could be tolerated. Story-writing was a genteel accomplishment and reflected credit upon the name. But leaving the paternal roof to wash other people's teacups, nurse other people's ails, and obey other people's orders for hire—this, this was degradation; and headstrong Louisa would disgrace her name forever if she did it.

Opposition only fired the revolutionary blood in my veins, and I crowned my iniquity by the rebellious declaration:

"If doing this work hurts my respectability, I wouldn't give much for it. My aristocratic ancestors don't feed or clothe me and my democratic ideas of honesty and honor won't let me be idle or dependent. You need not know me if you are ashamed of me, and I won't ask you for a penny; so, if I never do succeed in anything, I shall have the immense satisfaction of knowing I am under no obligation to any one."

In spite of the laughter and the lamentation, I got ready my small wardrobe, consisting of two calico dresses and one delaine, made by myself, also several large and uncompromising blue aprons and three tidy little sweeping-caps; for I had some English notions about housework and felt that my muslin hair-protectors would be useful in some of the "light labors" I was to undertake. It is needless to say they were very becoming. Then, firmly embracing my family, I set forth, one cold January day, with my little trunk, a stout heart, and a five-dollar bill for my fortune.

"She will be back in a week," was my sister's prophecy, as she wiped her weeping eye.

"No, she won't, for she has promised to stay the month out and she will keep her word," answered my mother, who always defended the black sheep of her flock.

I heard both speeches, and registered a tremendous vow to keep that promise, if I died in the attempt—little dreaming, poor innocent, what lay before me.

Josephus meantime had written me several remarkable letters, describing the different members of the family I was about to enter. His account was peculiar, but I believed every word of it and my romantic fancy was much excited by the details he gave. The principal ones are as follows, condensed from the voluminous epistles which he evidently enjoyed writing:

"You will find a stately mansion, fast falling to decay, for my father will have nothing repaired, preferring that the old house and its master should crumble away together. I have, however, been permitted to rescue a few rooms from ruin; and here I pass my recluse life, surrounded by the things I love. This will naturally be more attractive to you than the gloomy apartments my father inhabits, and I hope you will here allow me to minister to your young and cheerful nature when your daily cares are over. I need such companionship and shall always welcome you to my abode.

"Eliza, my sister, is a child at forty, for she has lived alone with my father and an old servant all her life. She is a good creature, but not lively, and needs stirring up, as you will soon see. Also I hope by your means to rescue her from the evil influence of Puah, who, in my estimation, is a *wretch*. She has gained entire control over Eliza, and warps her mind with great skill, prejudicing her against *me* and thereby desolating my home. Puah hates *me* and always has. Why I know not, except that I will not yield to her control. She ruled here for years while I was away, and my return upset all her nefarious plans. It will always be my firm opinion that she has tried to *poison me*, and may again. But even this dark suspicion will not deter me from my duty. I cannot send her away, for both my deluded father and my sister have entire faith in her, and I cannot shake it. She is faithful and kind to them, so I submit and remain to guard them, even at the risk of my life.

"I tell you these things because I wish you to know all and be warned, for this old hag has a specious tongue, and I should grieve to see you deceived by her lies. Say nothing, but watch her silently, and help me to thwart her evil plots; but do not trust her, or beware."

Now this was altogether romantic and sensational, and I felt as if about to enter one of those delightfully dangerous houses we read of in novels, where perils, mysteries, and sins freely disport themselves, till the newcomer sets all to rights, after unheard of trials and escapes.

I arrived at twilight, just the proper time for the heroine to appear; and, as no one answered my modest solo on the rusty knocker, I walked in and looked about me. Yes, here was the long, shadowy hall, where the ghosts doubtless walked at midnight. Peering in at an open door on the right, I saw a parlor full of ancient furniture, faded, dusty, and dilapidated. Old portraits stared at me from the walls and a damp chill froze the marrow of my bones in the most approved style.

"The romance opens well," I thought, and, peeping in at an opposite door, beheld a luxurious apartment, full of the warm glow of firelight, the balmy breath of hyacinths and roses, the white glimmer of piano keys, and tempting rows of books along the walls.

The contrast between the two rooms was striking, and, after an admiring survey, I continued my explorations, thinking that I should not mind being "ministered to" in that inviting place when my work was done.

A third door showed me a plain, dull sitting room, with an old man napping in his easy-chair. I heard voices in the kitchen beyond, and, entering there, beheld Puah the fiend. Unfortunately, for the dramatic effect of the tableaux, all I saw was a mild-faced old woman, buttering toast, while she conversed with her familiar, a comfortable gray cat.

The old lady greeted me kindly, but I fancied her faded blue eye had a weird expression and her amiable words were all a snare, though I own I was rather disappointed at the commonplace appearance of this humble Borgia.

She showed me to a tiny room, where I felt more like a young giantess than ever, and was obliged to stow away my possessions as snugly as in a ship's cabin. When I presently descended, armed with a blue apron and "a heart for any fate," I found the old man awake and received from him a welcome full of ancient courtesy and kindliness. Miss Eliza crept in like a timid mouse, looking so afraid of her buxom companion that I forgot my own shyness in trying to relieve hers. She was so enveloped in shawls that all I could discover was that my mistress was a very nervous little woman, with a small button of pale hair on the outside of her head and the vaguest notions of work inside. A few spasmodic remarks and many awkward pauses brought me to teatime, when Josephus appeared, as tall, thin, and cadaverous as ever. After his arrival there was no more silence, for he preached all suppertime something in this agreeable style.

"My young friend, our habits, as you see, are of the simplest. We eat in the kitchen, and all together, in the primitive fashion; for it suits my father and saves labor. I could wish more order and elegance; but *my* wishes are not consulted and I submit. I live above these petty crosses, and, though my health suffers from bad cookery, I do not murmur. Only, I must say, in passing, that if you *will* make your battercakes green with saleratus, Puah, I shall feel it my duty to throw them out of the window. *I* am used to poison; but I cannot see the coals of this blooming girl's stomach destroyed, as mine have been. And, speaking of duties, I may as well mention to you, Louisa (I call you so in a truly fraternal spirit), that I like to find my study in order when I come down in the morning; for I often need a few moments of solitude before I face the daily annoyances of my life. I shall permit *you* to perform this light task, for *you* have some idea of order (I see it in the formation of your brow), and feel sure that *you* will respect the sanctuary of thought. Eliza is so blind she does not see dust, and Puah enjoys devastating the one poor refuge I can call my own this side the grave. We are all waiting for you, sir. My father keeps up the old formalities, you observe; and I endure them, though *my* views are more advanced."

The old gentleman hastily finished his tea and returned thanks, when his son stalked gloomily away, evidently oppressed with the burden of his wrongs, also, as I irreverently fancied, with the seven "green" flapjacks he had devoured during the sermon.

I helped wash up the cups, and during that domestic rite Puah chatted in what I should have considered a cheery, social way had I not been darkly warned against her wiles.

"You needn't mind half Josephus says, my dear. He likes to hear himself talk and always goes on so before folks. I sometimes thinks his books and new ideas have sort of muddled his wits, for he is as full of notions as a paper is of pins; and he gets dreadfully put out if we don't give in to 'em. But, gracious me! they are so redicklus sometimes and so selfish I can't allow him to make a fool of himself or plague Lizy. She don't dare to say her soul is her own; so I have to stand up for her. His pa don't know half his odd doings; for I try to keep the old gentleman comfortable and have to manage 'em all, which is not an easy job I do assure you."

I had a secret conviction that she was right, but did not commit myself in any way, and we joined the social circle in the sitting room. The prospect was not a lively one, for the old gentleman nodded behind his newspaper; Eliza, with her head pinned up in a little blanket, slumbered on the sofa, Puah fell to knitting silently; and the plump cat dozed under the stove. Josephus was visible, artistically posed in the luxurious recesses of his cell, with the light beaming on his thoughtful brow, as he pored over a large volume or mused with upturned eye.

Having nothing else to do, I sat and stared at him, till, emerging from a deep reverie, with an effective start, he became conscious of my existence and beckoned me to approach the "sanctuary of thought" with a dramatic waft of his large hand.

I went, took possession of an easy chair, and prepared myself for elegant conversation. I was disappointed, however; for Josephus showed me a list of his favorite dishes, sole fruit of all that absorbing thought, and, with an earnestness that flushed his saffron countenance, gave me hints as to the proper preparation of these delicacies.

I mildly mentioned that I was not a cook; but was effectually silenced by being reminded that I came to be generally useful, to take his sister's place, and see that the flame of life which burned so feebly in this earthly tabernacle was fed with proper fuel. Mince pies, Welsh rarebits, sausages, and strong coffee did not strike me as strictly spiritual fare; but I listened meekly and privately resolved to shift this awful responsibility to Puah's shoulders.

Detecting me in gape, after an hour of this high converse, he presented me with an overblown rose, which fell to pieces before I got out of the room, pressed my hand, and dismissed me with a fervent "God bless you, child. Don't forget the dropped eggs for breakfast."

I was up betimes next morning and had the study in perfect order before the recluse appeared, enjoying a good prowl among the books as I worked and becoming so absorbed that I forgot the eggs, till a gusty sigh startled me, and I beheld Josephus, in dressing gown and slippers, languidly surveying the scene.

"Nay, do not fly," he said, as I grasped my duster in guilty haste. "It pleases me to see you here and lends a sweet, domestic charm to my solitary room. I like that graceful cap, that housewifely apron, and I beg you to wear them often; for it refreshes my eye to see something tasteful, young, and womanly about me. Eliza makes a bundle of herself and Puah is simply detestable."

He sank languidly into a chair and closed his eyes, as if the mere thought of his enemy was too much for him. I took advantage of this momentary prostration to slip away, convulsed with laughter at the looks and words of this bald-headed sentimentalist.

After breakfast I fell to work with a will, eager to show my powers and glad to put things to rights, for many hard jobs had evidently been waiting for a stronger arm than Puah's and a more methodical head than Eliza's.

Everything was dusty, moldy, shiftless, and neglected, except the domain of Josephus. Up-stairs the paper was dropping from the walls, the ancient furniture was all more or less dilapidated, and every hold and corner was full of relics tucked away by Puah, who was a regular old magpie. Rats and mice reveled in the empty rooms and spiders wove their tapestry undisturbed, for the old man would have nothing altered or repaired and his part of the house was fast going to ruin.

I longed to have a grand "clearing up"; but was forbidden to do more than to keep things in livable order. On the whole, it was fortunate, for I soon found that my hands would be kept busy with the realms of Josephus, whose ethereal being shrank from dust, shivered at a cold breath, and needed much cosseting with dainty food, hot fires, soft beds, and endless service, else, as he expressed it, the frail reed would break.

I regret to say that a time soon came when I felt supremely indifferent as to the breakage, and very skeptical as to the fragility of a reed that ate, slept, dawdled, and scolded so energetically. The rose that fell to pieces so suddenly was a good symbol of the rapid disappearance of all the romantic delusions I had indulged in for a time. A week's acquaintance with the inmates of this odd house quite settled my opinion, and further developments only confirmed it.

Miss Eliza was a nonentity and made no more impression on me than a fly. The old gentleman passed his days in a placid sort of doze and took no notice of what went on about him. Puah had been a faithful drudge for years, and, instead of being a "wretch," was, as I soon satisfied myself, a motherly old soul, with no malice in her. The secret of Josephus's dislike was that the reverend tyrant ruled the house, and all obeyed him but Puah, who had nursed him as a baby, boxed his ears as a boy, and was not afraid of him even when he became a man and a minister. I soon repented of my first suspicions, and grew fond of her, for without my old gossip I should have fared ill when my day of tribulation came.

At first I innocently accepted the fraternal invitations to visit the study, feeling that when my day's work was done I earned a right to rest and read. But I soon found that this was not the idea. I was not to read; but to be read to. I was not to enjoy the flowers, pictures, fire, and books; but to keep them in order for my lord to enjoy. I was also to be a passive bucket, into which he was to pour all manner of philosophic, metaphysical, and sentimental rubbish. I was to serve his needs, soothe his sufferings, and sympathize with all his sorrows—be a galley slave, in fact.

As soon as I clearly understood this, I tried to put an end to it by shunning the study and never lingering there an instant after my work was done. But it availed little, for Josephus demanded much sympathy and was bound to have it. So he came and read poems while I washed dishes, discussed his pet problems all meal-times, and put reproachful notes under my door, in which were comically mingled complaints of neglect and orders for dinner.

I bore it as long as I could, and then freed my mind in a declaration of independence, delivered in the kitchen, where he found me scrubbing the hearth. It was not an impressive attitude for an orator, nor was the occupation one a girl would choose when receiving calls; but I have always felt grateful for the intense discomfort of that moment, since it gave me the courage to rebel outright. Stranded on a small island of mat, in a sea of soapsuds, I brandished a scrubbing brush, as I indignantly informed him that I came to be a companion to his sister, not to him, and I should keep that post or none. This I followed up by reproaching him with the delusive reports he had given me of the place and its duties, and assuring him that I should not stay long unless matters mended.

"But I offer you lighter tasks, and you refuse them," he began, still hovering in the doorway, whither he had hastily retired when I opened my batteries.

"But I don't like the tasks, and consider them much worse than hard work," was my ungrateful answer, as I sat upon my island, with the softsoap conveniently near.

"Do you mean to say you prefer to scrub the hearth to sitting in my charming room while I read Hegel to you?" he demanded, glaring down upon me.

"Infinitely," I responded promptly, and emphasized my words by beginning to scrub with a zeal that made the bricks white with foam.

"Is it possible!" and, with a groan at my depravity, Josephus retired, full of ungodly wrath.

I remember that I immediately burst into jocund song, so that no doubt might remain in his mind, and continued to warble cheerfully till my task was done. I also remember that I cried heartily when I got to my room, I was so vexed, disappointed, and tired. But my bower was so small I should soon have swamped the furniture if I had indulged copiously in tears; therefore I speedily dried them up, wrote a comic letter home, and waited with interest to see what would happen next.

Far be it from me to accuse one of the nobler sex of spite or the small revenge of underhand annoyances and slights to one who could not escape and would not retaliate; but after that day a curious change came over the spirit of that very unpleasant dream. Gradually all the work of the house had been slipping into my hands; for Eliza was too poorly to help and direct, and Puah too old to do much besides the cooking. About this time I found that even the roughest work was added to my share, for Josephus was unusually feeble and no one was hired to do his chores. Having made up my mind to go when the month was out, I said nothing, but dug paths, brought water from the well, split kindlings, made fires, and sifted ashes, like a true Cinderella.

There never had been any pretense of companionship with Eliza, who spent her days mulling over the fire, and seldom exerted herself except to find odd jobs for me to do—rusty knives to clean, sheets to turn, old stockings to mend, and, when all else failed, some paradise of moths and mice to be cleared up; for the house was full of such "glory holds."

If I remonstrated, Eliza at once dissolved into tears and said she must do as she was told; Puah begged me to hold on till spring, when things would be much better; and pity pleaded for the two poor souls. But I don't think I could have stood it if my promise had not bound me, for when the fiend said "Budge" honor said "Budge not" and I stayed.

But, being a mortal worm, I turned now and then when ireful Josephus trod upon me too hard, especially in the matter of boot-blacking. I really don't know why that is considered such humiliating work for a woman; but so it is, and there I drew the line. I would have cleaned the old man's shoes without a murmur; but he preferred to keep their native rustiness intact. Eliza never went out, and Puah affected carpet-slippers of the Chinese-junk pattern. Josephus, however, plumed himself upon his feet, which like his nose, were large, and never took his walks abroad without having his boots in a high state of polish. He had brushed them himself at first; but soon after the explosion I discovered a pair of muddy boots in the shed, set suggestively near the blacking-box. I did not take the hint; feeling instinctively that this amiable being was trying how much I would bear for the sake of peace.

The boots remained untouched; and another pair soon came to keep them company, whereat I smiled wickedly as I chopped just kindlings enough for my own use. Day after day the collection grew, and neither party gave in. Boots were succeeded by shoes, then rubbers gave a pleasing variety to the long line, and then I knew the end was near.

"Why are not my boots attended to?" demanded Josephus, one evening, when obliged to go out.

"I'm sure I don't know," was Eliza's helpless answer.

"I told Louizy I guessed you'd want some of 'em before long," observed Puah with an exasperating twinkle in her old eye.

"And what did she say?" asked my lord with an ireful whack of his velvet slippers as he cast them down.

"Oh! she said she was so busy doing your other work you'd have to do that yourself; and I thought she was about right."

"Louizy" heard it all through the slide, and could have embraced the old woman for her words, but kept still till Josephus had resumed his slippers with a growl and retired to the shed, leaving Eliza in tears, Puah chuckling, and the rebellious handmaid exulting in the china-closet.

Alas! for romance and the Christian virtues, several pairs of boots were cleaned that night, and my sinful soul enjoyed the spectacle of the reverend bootblack at his task. I even found my "fancy work," as I called the evening job of paring a bucketful of hard russets with a dull knife, much cheered by the shoe-brush accompaniment played in the shed.

Thunder-clouds rested upon the martyr's brow at breakfast, and I was as much ignored as the cat. And what a relief that was! The piano was locked up, so were the bookcases, the newspapers mysteriously disappeared, and a solemn silence reigned at table, for no one dared to talk when that gifted tongue was mute. Eliza fled from the gathering storm and had a comfortable fit of neuralgia in her own room, where Puah nursed her, leaving me to skirmish with the enemy.

It was not a fair fight, and that experience lessened my respect for mankind immensely. I did my best, however—grubbed about all day and amused my dreary evenings as well as I could; too proud even to borrow a book, lest it should seem like a surrender. What a long month it was, and how eagerly I counted the hours of that last week, for my time was up Saturday and I hoped to be off at once. But when I announced my intention such dismay fell upon Eliza that my heart was touched, and Puah so urgently begged me to stay till they could get some one that I consented to remain a few days longer, and wrote posthaste to my mother, telling her to send a substitute quickly or I should do something desperate.

That blessed woman, little dreaming of all the woes I had endured, advised me to be patient, to do the generous thing, and be sure I should not regret it in the end. I groaned, submitted, and did regret it all the days of my life.

Three mortal weeks I waited; for, though two other victims came, I was implored to set them going, and tried to do it. But both fled after a day or two, condemning the place as a very hard one and calling me a fool to stand it another hour. I entirely agreed with them on both points, and, when I had cleared up after the second incapable lady, I tarried not for the coming of a third, but clutched my property and announced my departure by the next train.

Of course, Eliza wept, Puah moaned, the old man politely regretted, and the younger one washed his hands of the whole affair by shutting himself up in his room and forbidding me to say farewell because "he could not bear it." I laughed, and fancied it done for effect then; but I soon understood it better and did not laugh.

At the last moment, Eliza nervously tucked a sixpenny pocketbook into my hand and shrouded herself in the little blanket with a sob. But Puah kissed me kindly and whispered, with an odd look: "Don't blame us for anything. Some folks is liberal and some ain't." I thanked the poor old soul for her kindness to me and trudged gayly away to the station, whither my property had preceded me on a wheelbarrow, hired at my own expense.

I never shall forget that day. A bleak March afternoon, a sloppy, lonely road, and one hoarse crow stalking about a field, so like Josephus that I could not resist throwing a snowball at him. Behind me stood the dull old house, no longer either mysterious or romantic in my disenchanted eyes; before me rumbled the barrow, bearing my dilapidated wardrobe; and in my pocket reposed what I fondly hoped was, if not a liberal, at least an honest return for seven weeks of the hardest work I ever did.

Unable to resist the desire to see what my earnings were, I opened the purse and beheld *four dollars.*

I have had a good many bitter minutes in my life; but one of the bitterest came to me as I stood there in the windy road, with the sixpenny pocket-book open before me, and looked from my poor chapped, grimy, chill-blained hands to the paltry sum that was considered reward enough for all the hard and humble labor they had done.

A girl's heart is a sensitive thing. And mine had been very full lately; for it had suffered many of the trials that wound deeply yet cannot be told; so I think it as but natural that my first impulse was to go straight back to that sacred study and fling this insulting money at the feet of him who sent it. But I was so boiling over with indignation that I could not trust myself in his presence, lest I should be unable to resist the temptation to shake him, in spite of his cloth.

No, I would go home, show my honorable wounds, tell my pathetic tale, and leave my parents to avenge my wrongs. I did so; but over that harrowing scene I drop a veil, for my feeble pen refuses to depict the emotions of my outraged family. I will merely mention that the four dollars went back and the reverend Josephus never heard the last of it in that neighborhood.

My experiment seemed a dire failure and I mourned it as such for years; but more than once in my life I have been grateful for that serio-comico experience, since it has taught me many lessons. One of the most useful of these has been the power of successfully making a companion, not a servant, of those whose aid I need, and helping to gild their honest wages with the sympathy and justice which can sweeten the humblest and lighten the hardest task.

DOVER · THRIFT · EDITIONS

All books complete and unabridged. All 5³⁄₁₆″ × 8¼″, paperbound.
Just $1.00–$2.00 in U.S.A.

POETRY

GREAT LOVE POEMS, Shane Weller (ed.). 128pp. 27284-2 $1.00
SELECTED POEMS, Walt Whitman. 128pp. 26878-0 $1.00
THE BALLAD OF READING GAOL AND OTHER POEMS, Oscar Wilde. 64pp. 27072-6 $1.00
FAVORITE POEMS, William Wordsworth. 80pp. 27073-4 $1.00
EARLY POEMS, William Butler Yeats. 128pp. 27808-5 $1.00

FICTION

FLATLAND: A ROMANCE OF MANY DIMENSIONS, Edwin A. Abbott. 96pp. 27263-X $1.00
BEOWULF, Beowulf (trans. by R. K. Gordon). 64pp. 27264-8 $1.00
CIVIL WAR STORIES, Ambrose Bierce. 128pp. 28038-1 $1.00
ALICE'S ADVENTURES IN WONDERLAND, Lewis Carroll. 96pp. 27543-4 $1.00
O PIONEERS!, Willa Cather. 128pp. 27785-2 $1.00
FIVE GREAT SHORT STORIES, Anton Chekhov. 96pp. 26463-7 $1.00
FAVORITE FATHER BROWN STORIES, G. K. Chesterton. 96pp. 27545-0 $1.00
THE AWAKENING, Kate Chopin. 128pp. 27786-0 $1.00
HEART OF DARKNESS, Joseph Conrad. 80pp. 26464-5 $1.00
THE SECRET SHARER AND OTHER STORIES, Joseph Conrad. 128pp. 27546-9 $1.00
THE OPEN BOAT AND OTHER STORIES, Stephen Crane. 128pp. 27547-7 $1.00
THE RED BADGE OF COURAGE, Stephen Crane. 112pp. 26465-3 $1.00
A CHRISTMAS CAROL, Charles Dickens. 80pp. 26865-9 $1.00
THE CRICKET ON THE HEARTH AND OTHER CHRISTMAS STORIES, Charles Dickens. 128pp. 28039-X $1.00
NOTES FROM THE UNDERGROUND, Fyodor Dostoyevsky. 96pp. 27053-X $1.00
SIX GREAT SHERLOCK HOLMES STORIES, Sir Arthur Conan Doyle. 112pp. 27055-6 $1.00
WHERE ANGELS FEAR TO TREAD, E. M. Forster. 128pp. (Available in U.S. only) 27791-7 $1.00
THE OVERCOAT AND OTHER SHORT STORIES, Nikolai Gogol. 112pp. 27057-2 $1.00
GREAT GHOST STORIES, John Grafton (ed.). 112pp. 27270-2 $1.00
THE LUCK OF ROARING CAMP AND OTHER SHORT STORIES, Bret Harte. 96pp. 27271-0 $1.00
THE SCARLET LETTER, Nathaniel Hawthorne. 192pp. 28048-9 $2.00
YOUNG GOODMAN BROWN AND OTHER SHORT STORIES, Nathaniel Hawthorne. 128pp. 27060-2 $1.00
THE GIFT OF THE MAGI AND OTHER SHORT STORIES, O. Henry. 96pp. 27061-0 $1.00
THE NUTCRACKER AND THE GOLDEN POT, E. T. A. Hoffmann. 128pp. 27806-9 $1.00
THE BEAST IN THE JUNGLE AND OTHER STORIES, Henry James. 128pp. 27552-3 $1.00
THE TURN OF THE SCREW, Henry James. 96pp. 26684-2 $1.00
DUBLINERS, James Joyce. 160pp. 26870-5 $1.00
A PORTRAIT OF THE ARTIST AS A YOUNG MAN, James Joyce. 192pp. 28050-0 $2.00